Carrie stared at the phone, hesitated, then lifted it to her ear and said hello.

Seconds ticked by. Three. Four. Five.

In disgust, she lowered the phone and poised her forefinger over the end button.

"Don't hang up." The harsh, low whisper effectively masked the caller's voice. "Not yet."

"Who is this?" she demanded.

"Don't matter." His low, venomous laugh grated against her skin and raised the hair at the back of her neck. "Not yet."

"Billy?"

He ignored her question. "You look pretty tonight."

Her hand shook and she nearly dropped the phone. "What?"

"Real pretty."

"Who is this?"

"I'd be more careful in the future if I was you. The night isn't all that safe."

"Maybe not for you, either," she snapped. She jammed a shaking finger onto the keypad of the phone to end the call. He'd been *watching* her....

Books by Roxanne Rustand

Love Inspired Suspense

*Hard Evidence
*Vendetta
*Wildfire
Deadly Competition
**Final Exposure
**Fatal Burn
**End Game
**Murder at Granite Falls

*Snow Canyon Ranch
**Big Sky Secrets

Love Inspired

*Winter Reunion
*Aspen Creek Crossroads

ROXANNE RUSTAND

lives in the country with her husband and a menagerie of pets, many of whom find their way into her books. She works part-time as a registered dietitian at a psychiatric facility, but otherwise you'll find her writing at home in her jammies, surrounded by three dogs begging for treats, or out in the barn with the horses. Her favorite time of all is when her kids are home—though all three are now busy with college and jobs.

This is her twenty-fifth novel. *RT Book Reviews* nominated her for a Career Achievement Award in 2005, and she won the magazine's award for Best Superromance of 2006.

She loves to hear from readers! Her snail-mail address is P.O. Box 2550, Cedar Rapids, Iowa, 52406-2550. You can also contact her at: www.roxannerustand.com, www.shoutlife.com/roxannerustand, or at her blog, where readers and writers talk about their pets: www.roxannerustand.blogspot.com.

MURDER
AT
GRANITE
FALLS

Roxanne Rustand

Love Inspired

Recycling programs
for this product may
not exist in your area.

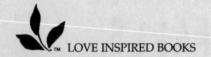 LOVE INSPIRED BOOKS

ISBN-13: 978-0-373-67457-2

MURDER AT GRANITE FALLS

Copyright © 2011 by Roxanne Rustand

www.LoveInspiredBooks.com

Printed in U.S.A.

Even though I walk through the valley of the shadow of death, I will fear no evil, for Thou are with me, Thy rod and thy staff, they comfort me.

—*Psalms* 23:4

With love to my dear mother, Arline,
and brother Glen; and to Larry, who has been
so supportive during my writing journey.

ONE

Tightening her grip on the steering wheel, Carrie Randall glanced again in her rearview mirror. *The vehicle was still behind her.* Billy? It couldn't be. She'd been so very, very careful.

She'd caught a better glimpse of the car while negotiating a set of hairpin turns at a higher elevation. Not close enough to identify the make and model. But close enough to be fairly certain it was the same one that had tailed her for the past two hours.

She palmed her cell phone, checking the number of reception bars on the screen. *Zero.* No surprise in this isolated part of the Montana Rockies, where bears probably outnumbered the two-footed residents three-to-one.

She frowned at the odometer. Ten miles to the town of Granite Falls. The lane leading to her new home should be coming up in less than a mile. But if her ex-husband was following her, the last thing she wanted was to lead him right to her door.

An earsplitting yowl erupted from the cage on the seat behind her, followed by the frantic scrabbling of paws. "It's okay, Harley. Just hang on."

She stepped on the gas and rocketed past the little gravel lane that wound into the pines off to the left. Then she headed straight for town.

Granite Falls was as picturesque as its tourism website claimed.

The mountain highway widened into a charming six-block-long main street flanked on both sides by historic storefronts, boardwalks and hitching rails straight out of an old Western movie. The center of town was filled with upscale shops and quaint restaurants geared to the tourist trade, while the dusty pickups nosed up to the feed store and café on the far edge of town revealed where the locals gathered. Would that be a safe place to stop?

A maroon Lawler County sheriff's deputy patrol car parked face-out in front of the café made her decision easy.

She checked in her rearview mirror once more, turned sharply into the parking lot and pulled up along the cruiser. Over her shoulder, she saw the dark sedan slow down, then speed past. *Good riddance.*

If she lingered in town long enough, the driver might give up, or get careless and not see her leave. Though if it was Billy, he'd be back, restraining order or not.

"Howdy, ma'am."

She turned to find a burly deputy behind her, a foam coffee cup in his hand, waiting to get into his car. The silver name badge pinned to his khaki uniform breast pocket identified him as Vance Munson.

Perhaps in his late thirties, he'd probably been hot stuff in high school in an Elvis sort of way, until he'd put on some years and packed on an extra fifty pounds. With an affable smile on his face, a rumpled uniform and a cellophane bag of cookies in his hand, he reminded her of a genial teddy bear.

"Sorry." She stepped back to give him space. "I... was a little distracted. I thought someone was following me on the highway."

The deputy's full lips quirked into a smile. "You'll find a lot of tourists in these parts, headin' into town just like yourself. No cause for worry."

"I'm actually moving here." She extended her arm, and he juggled his coffee cup into his other hand to accept the handshake. "Carrie Randall."

He rocked back on his heels, taking her measure. "Welcome, then."

"A dark sedan followed me for the past hundred miles then right into town." She looked up the empty Main Street. "Though I couldn't tell you the license plate or even the make of the car."

"Like I said, you'll find a lot of travelers out here on long trips. Destinations are few and far between.

People go sightseeing, and you might run into the same folks time and again. No call for worry."

She eyed a family coming out of the café and lowered her voice. "I had to file a restraining order against my ex-husband last year."

Munson's gaze sharpened. "Well, now," he drawled. "That might be a calf of a different color. He knows you're moving here?"

"I certainly didn't tell him. I hear he's following a rodeo circuit down in the Southwest this summer. But…"

"But you aren't sure." Munson tipped his head toward the center of town. "Ma'am, you can find the county courthouse just four blocks west of here. You might want to file here, as well."

"Well…"

"It's for your own good." He gave her a warm, encouraging smile. "Where are you staying? I can pass the word along. We like to keep an eye on things around here."

Billy had dropped out of sight during the past year, while she stayed with her protective brother, Trace. During that time, she'd felt safe from Billy's volatile temper, which had escalated ever since their divorce.

Now, she just wanted to start life fresh, with none of those old reminders. No looking over her shoulder. And no rumors filtering out about her being another one of those women who had fallen for charm and flash and ended up in an abusive relationship with an unfaithful man. In small towns like this one, idle talk by one of Lawler County's finest would reach the local grapevine and she'd be branded forever. "I—I'll be fine."

A flicker of annoyance crossed Munson's expression. "Too many women fail to ask for help, ma'am, and the results can be mighty sad. Our sheriff's department will do whatever it can to assist you, but you have to cooperate."

She sighed. "I have a summer lease on an upstairs apartment out at Wolf River Rafting Company."

"The Bradleys," he said, his mouth twisting with a hint of distaste.

He'd settled his aviator shades into place, but from his long silence and the muscle ticking along his jaw, she guessed that the deputy didn't approve. "Is there something I should know?"

"Just…watch your step out there." He hesitated, as if he wanted to say more, but then he shook his head. "And don't ever forget to lock your doors."

With Vance Munson's words still playing through her thoughts, Carrie felt a shiver of unease as she stepped out of her aging silver Tahoe and shielded her eyes against the setting sun.

Sure enough, Wolf River Rafting Company was emblazoned in gilt letters on a sign over the door of the two-story log building overlooking the river and on the smaller, matching building next to the riverbank.

This would be her home for the next three months, and she'd been lucky to find it through a chance discovery on the internet, though as she surveyed the area, a chill worked its way down her spine. The small clearing was bounded on one side by river, on the other three by impenetrable pine forest, and to the west the massive, snowcapped Rockies loomed high along the horizon.

She should've expected a Montana Rockies rafting company would be located in an isolated place offering good access to a river, but she could see *nothing* else close by. Not a store, not a resort. Not even a cabin. And it was a good half mile off the highway, well out of sight of any passing traffic.

Which meant she'd probably be totally alone come nightfall. *Vulnerable.*

Was that why the deputy had seemed hesitant about her moving out here? The tense knot in her stomach started to relax. Maybe that was it—he hadn't been hinting at any concern about the Bradleys. He just thought this place would be terribly isolated for a woman living by herself.

Though right now, cheerful pandemonium reigned. A jumble of dirt bikes had been ditched against the trees by a group of mud-streaked boys fishing along the shore. They were fairly bursting with energy, jostling each other and teasing, and then one fell in the water and the rest laughed uproariously when he emerged.

Carrie smiled, remembering the exquisite patience

and silence of fly-fishing with Trace. Any fish within a hundred yards of these kids had probably long since skedaddled.

To the right, a couple of eight-man white-water rafts were pulled up on the grass. Down at the river's edge, a dozen silver-haired women chattered on the rocky bank next to a massive rubber raft—a twenty-footer, probably—with inflated tubular sides. The customers were fumbling with the fastenings of their bulky orange life vests while a tall, younger woman moved among them, redirecting wayward straps and snugging the vests into position. Occasionally, she darted into the log boathouse to fetch a different size.

The scene brought back happy memories of the river guiding job Carrie had held through college. It all seemed so normal. So safe.

The woman in charge studied her for a split second, then hiked her thumb toward the building. "Logan's inside," she shouted.

Carrie nodded, hit the lock button on her key chain out of habit, and picked her way across the river rock.

At the corner of the building she abruptly came face-to-chest with a man in a faded Denver Broncos T-shirt and khaki cargo shorts.

He caught her upper arms with his strong hands, steadied her, then released his grip. "Kayak rental?"

At his touch, an expected sense of awareness

warmed her heart, and she quelled a sudden flash of panic. Her immediate instinct was to run.

After a heartbeat, she managed a smile and looked up into the bluest eyes she'd ever seen this side of Paul Newman on the silver screen. *Oh, my.*

"Sorry," she mumbled, catching her breath.

"My fault."

"I—I'm Carrie Randall. I'm here about the apartment."

His face registered a flash of surprise, and from his quick, searching look, she knew he was probably thinking she was some harebrained city gal, way out of her element.

"Well, then," he drawled as he tipped his head toward an open staircase on the side of the building. "Let's do the tour. I'm Logan Bradley, by the way."

His face was lean and tan, with a strong jaw and a shock of near-black hair tumbling over his forehead that made him look as though he belonged on some back lot in Hollywood, not here in the middle of nowhere.

He offered his hand for a brief shake, the warmth of his fingers settling in the vicinity of her heart and setting off alarm bells that she would not ignore. *Charmer...charmer...*

She blinked and abruptly jerked her hand back.

This instant, blinding reaction was exactly what had drawn her to Billy, and the emotional wreckage from their divorce was still too painful to bear.

Though fortunately, her concerns about that dark sedan appeared to be unfounded. Deputy Munson had probably been right about it belonging to some vacationer following the same long, long highway on the way to Granite Falls. No one had been lying in wait when she left town. No one had followed her here. *Thank You, Lord.*

Logan frowned at her. By now, he had to figure she was not only a city slicker, but a fruitcake to boot, if she could barely shake his hand. He was probably even having serious second thoughts about accepting his new lodger.

Not a good thing.

If he changed his mind, the newest teacher in Granite Falls would be sleeping in her Tahoe during summer term, because there was literally nowhere else in the area that wasn't priced for the affluent tourist trade. Isolated or not, this was her one shot for a roof over her head this summer, and she had no other choice.

"The apartment?" she prodded, pinning on her brightest smile.

He seemed to shake off his thoughts, and with a long sigh he led the way up a rustic outside stairway to a balcony that ran the length of the building.

Two doors, one at either end, stood open to the warm afternoon sun reflecting off the river. Between them, six double-hung windows were raised to catch the soft, pine-scented breeze.

He tipped his head toward the woman now

shepherding the flock of older women into the raft. "My sister, Penny, is the assistant manager here. She lives in town, but she's out here almost every day." He cracked a lopsided smile. "She came up and aired your place out this morning and checked for spiders and mice, just so you wouldn't have any surprises."

Given the intent gleam in his eyes, she wondered if he was hoping she'd just head straight back to town. He couldn't know that a few little guests were the least of her worries.

She lifted a shoulder. "Not a problem. I've got Harley with me."

His thick, dark lashes—it was so unfair, when a guy was blessed with what she couldn't even manage with mascara—lowered as he gave her a narrowed look. *"Harley?"*

She waved an airy hand at him as she passed and stepped into the apartment. "He'll dispatch anything that moves, believe me."

At least it was true for small vermin. If her raggedy old tomcat could handle the two-legged kind, she'd feel a whole lot safer.

Logan ushered her into the apartment and she caught her breath in delight as she stepped inside.

The photos on the internet realty listing hadn't done justice to the feeling of being up in the tree-tops, with the pine paneled walls and abundance of sunshine pouring in the windows.

A bright crazy quilt hung on the wall above a ruby

plush sofa and two matching upholstered chairs perfect for curling up with a good book. The L-shaped kitchen offered ample counter space with gleaming stainless-steel appliances that looked almost new. A gold, ruby and forest-green area rug warmed the hardwood floors.

"This is absolutely lovely. I wasn't expecting it to be so nice."

A half smile briefly touched Logan's mouth. "Penny probably had a little too much fun with this. You have it for the summer, then a group of skiers has reserved it for over the winter. After that, she plans to live here during the tourist season every summer."

Again, that little frisson of worry started to tie Carrie's stomach into a knot. "So you don't live on the property, either?"

"Penny stays with our great-aunt in town and I have an old cabin a quarter mile upriver. At least one of us is here from sunrise until dark…most days. Though I'm on the road at times, as well."

"Sounds like a busy schedule."

He lifted a shoulder. "Penny and I are just getting the raft business going again after a few…setbacks last year. Eventually, she'll manage it and I'll start adding an outfitting business for trips up into the mountains."

She nodded, hiding her dismay at his words. She *would* be alone here.

Though no one knew exactly where she'd moved,

except for her brother and his fiancée, and she'd carefully kept his ranch as her cell phone and credit card billing address since she could pay her bills online. With that and no home ownership records to trace, it would be hard for Billy or anyone else from her past to find her.

Surely everything would be fine.

But still, as she followed Logan down the stairs to go after her luggage, she started to pray.

"So what do you think?" Penny's mouth twitched as she looked up at the top floor of the building, where their new tenant was busily sweeping off the balcony. "Will the new teacher last out here?"

Logan snorted. "My guess? Not even as long as the past two tenants."

"I don't know…she sounded pretty desperate for a place to rent over the summer."

"That's what the others said. A little problem with bears in the trash cans at night and a few wolf howls sent them both packing in a hurry. I gave her our cell phone numbers to call, in case she gets spooked about something."

His gaze strayed to the petite woman wielding the broom. She had to be a good six inches shorter than Penny's five foot eight, and with that gleaming cap of short mahogany hair and those sparkling hazel eyes, she looked like an energetic pixie. When she'd mentioned that she had some guy named Harley with her, he'd even felt a flash of serious disappointment that she was committed to someone…

Until he'd discovered that Harley was probably the most battered, disreputable cat he'd ever seen.

"I'm not a betting man, but I'll give her two days, tops. When we ran into each other at the corner of the building she was as skittish as a week-old filly."

"Must have been all of your charisma," Penny teased.

"Or maybe she heard the rumors and believes them. I hope not—we'll need her rent money if we have a slow summer like the last one."

Penny's smile faded. "That won't happen. Things have died down around here, haven't they?"

"We can hope." He lifted a shoulder. "I just want everything in place for you here so I can get back on the road as soon as possible."

She paled. "Are you sure that's a good idea? Your doctor said—"

"I won't take chances." He ruffled the top of her wavy russet mane, which had long since escaped her attempts at a ponytail, just as he had when they were kids growing up on a ranch.

She batted his hand away. "And you think riding saddle broncs isn't taking a chance?"

"If I don't pay off those short-term loans from last year, we could lose this place. I've got to go."

"We'll figure out something. It isn't worth it, Logan."

"But you own a quarter of this business and you'll go down if I do. I can't let that happen."

She nudged him in the ribs and made a face. "I think it's an excuse to leave town and not enjoy that lovely cabin any longer."

He laughed at that. "I'm getting to know the mice on a first-name basis. You can move into the spare room any time you want—they'd love to meet you."

She rolled her eyes. "Great offer. I'll think about it awhile longer, though."

"At least you're staying with Aunt Betty. I think she actually has a *furnace* there, if I'm not mistaken. And plumbing that works. All the time."

"She already asked you to move in, too. There's plenty of room."

At the thought of all the lace and frills in Betty's house, Logan shuddered. The second guest room was done in lilac and pink, with an explosion of flowers on the wallpaper, and though Betty was a sweetheart, she loved to hover and fuss.

"I'm fine with where I'm at for now. All I need is to get back on the circuit for the rest of this season and then the next, draw good broncs at every rodeo, and not part ways with any of them until the eight-second buzzer. Then I promise I'll quit for good."

They both fell silent for a moment, and he knew they were thinking about the same thing—the accusations and ensuing trial that had nearly ruined

Logan's reputation and the beginnings of their rafting company last year.

The legal costs had taken his savings, but at least he'd had good representation. Without it, he would've been behind bars…maybe for the rest of his life.

"I'm going to hold you to that promise," she murmured. "If it means throwing you in the boathouse and tossing away the key."

"I'd sure be a lot of use in there."

"Speaking of that, I had a really good group today. Those Red Hat ladies are the best." Penny blew a stray wisp of hair out of her eyes. "And we've already got some reservations booked well into June, so we've got a good start on the season. I think the new website has helped a lot."

"Agreed."

"We'll be fine, Logan." She rested a hand on his forearm. "People will forget about what happened. They'll realize you couldn't possibly be capable of hurting anyone."

"Maybe." He steeled himself, waiting for one of her platitudes about turning his burdens over to God, but she'd probably given up on trying to convince him. He hoped so.

Up on the outside balcony, Carrie stood at the door to her apartment. "Thanks again for helping move my things in," she called out.

Logan lifted a hand in reply, and she waved as she turned to go back inside.

There were good reasons for getting back on the road, and now a new one had just moved into the apartment above the rafting office.

Sweet, perky, with an infectious smile and an endearing hint of vulnerability, Carrie reminded him of Janie, the love of his life through high school and college, and he could almost envy the kids who were going to be in Carrie's classroom every day.

Penny followed his glance at the balcony, then angled an amused smile at him. "This is sure going to be an interesting summer."

He leveled an impatient look at her. "Don't you have something important to do?"

"Nope. Seriously, it's time you got on with your life. Just because things didn't work out with Lorena shouldn't be reason to end up a hermit."

"A hermit," he retorted.

"Well, nearly." Penny's eyes danced. "You're already thirty-three, so old age is just around the corner. It's time to move on."

Even after two years, Penny wanted to comfort him over the failed relationship with his longtime girlfriend, but long before that—when Penny had been too young to fully understand what was going on—he'd had a far bigger loss. Part of him had died with Janie the day a semi T-boned her car, and he'd never been the same.

Maybe Lorena was right.

Maybe his past had turned him into just another emotionless, thoughtless guy who wasn't capable of commitment. But at least that way, he didn't ever risk breaking the remnants of his heart.

The last rays of sunshine were slicing through the mountains to the west when Carrie finally finished putting away her clothes and arranging her possessions. Logan and his sister had left an hour ago, after stopping in to make sure she was settling in, and they'd also made sure that she had their cell numbers and the home number of their aunt Betty who lived in town.

Nice people, both of them. At least on the surface. *Or were they?*

Her stomach tensed into a tight ball of anxiety once again, because she still could not set aside that brief conversation with the deputy in town. There had been *distaste* in his expression when she'd announced her destination—far more than she might have expected if he just felt concern about a woman alone coming to this isolated place.

She shook off her doubts with a heavenward glance.

She'd prayed long and hard about the decision to come to this town. It was time to reestablish her independence and her career. She'd done the right thing, and worrying was a waste of time. But still…

Harley, curled up on the back of the sofa, opened one eye and looked at her, then went back to sleep, clearly unconcerned. "A *dog* would care," she said drily, stroking his soft fur. "He'd come and sit by me and offer moral support."

A deep rumble vibrated through the old cat's body—more junkyard engine than purr—letting her know that at least the most important creature in the room was content. Smiling to herself, she stepped out onto the balcony and braced her hands on the railing to lean out into the fresh, sweet pine-scented mountain air.

The rushing sounds of the Wolf River beckoned. Not more than a dozen yards from her new home, its closest bank offered an easy slope for beaching rafts. Even here, she could smell the water and damp earth. The water, now ink-black in the deepening twilight, brought back such good memories of her college summers....

Drawn to its wild beauty, she went down the outside stairs and took a few steps toward the river. The sound of a twig snapping jerked her to a halt as an invisible hand of fear grabbed at her shoulder. Prickles of awareness at the back of her neck escalated to absolute certainty. She was not alone.

Someone was here. Very, very close.

She could sense his eyes burning into her back.

Hear his breathing.

She could feel his heartbeat, pounding in cadence with her own. *Oh, Lord—I could really use Your help here.*

Stifling a cry, she whirled and flew up the stairs, flung open the door and slammed it shut as soon as she made it inside. Her heart hammered against her ribs and her lungs burned as she drove the dead bolt home, shoved the sofa against the door, then locked all the windows and pulled the shades.

No footsteps crept up the stairs.

Nothing was moving outside when she surreptitiously peeked through all of her windows. "Just my overactive imagination," she chastised herself aloud. "And next, I'll be afraid of dust bunnies." Maybe her "stalker" had just been a coyote, frozen in place at her unexpected appearance. Or a menacing chipmunk.

She'd finally talked herself down from that shaking, adrenaline-laced moment of fear when the cell phone clutched in her damp palm started to sing the first tinny notes of "Beer Barrel Polka." The screen listed only Unavailable Number and no name, so it wasn't anyone listed in her phonebook.

She stared at the phone, hesitated, then lifted it to her ear and said hello.

Seconds ticked by. *Three. Four. Five.*

In disgust, she lowered the phone and poised her forefinger over the end button.

"Don't hang up." The harsh, low whisper effectively masked the caller's voice. "Not yet."

"Who is this?" she demanded.

"Don't matter." His low, venomous laugh grated against her skin and raised the hair at the back of her neck. "Not yet."

"Billy?"

He ignored her question. "You look pretty in that green shirt tonight."

Her hand shook and she nearly dropped the phone. "What?"

"Real pretty."

"Who is this?"

"I'd be more careful in the future if I was you. The night isn't all that safe."

"Maybe not for you, either," she snapped. She jammed her finger onto the keypad of the phone to end the call.

So the sense that someone was out there hadn't been her imagination—and it definitely hadn't been some sort of wildlife, either. He'd been out there in the shadows. Watching *her.* Close enough to see the color of her shirt despite the deep twilight.

Billy?

He'd been her first guess, and a flash of anger and their long, troubled history had made her issue that foolish challenge. But now she wasn't so sure. And how could he or anyone else have found her new cell number?

Anxiety spider-crawled its way up her spine as she started pacing the confines of her apartment, her arms wrapped around her stomach. She'd given it only to her brother, Logan and to the school where she'd be working. That deputy had sure hinted at his opinion of the Bradleys. *Logan?* But why would he want to drive away a new tenant? It made no sense.

She debated about calling 911, or her brother, but he was far away with heavy responsibilities of his own. Or Logan himself, which might not be a bad idea.

He answered on the fifth ring, his voice laced with concern. "Something wrong?"

She chose her words carefully. "I hope I didn't interrupt anything."

"I'm at my aunt's house fixing a faucet."

Yeah, right. "This late?"

A pause. "I didn't have time until now." He sounded vaguely distracted. "Do you need something?"

Now she could hear faint female voices in the background and the clank of something metal—maybe a wrench—so he was telling the truth after all.

At least she hadn't confronted him face-to-face, where he'd see the warm flush of embarrassment creeping up her neck.

"Did…you or Penny give my phone number to anyone?"

A pause. "Of course not. Why?"

"Only a few people have it. I think I had a prowler."

"Did you call the sheriff?"

"I didn't actually see anyone, and there wasn't a crime." *Yet,* she thought with a shudder. "But a bit later I got a phone call—it had to be the same guy. No specific threat, but it was creepy."

"I can be there in twenty minutes. Keep your doors locked."

"You don't have to come. I just wanted to…um… mention it."

This time, the pause was much longer. "You wondered where I was tonight," he said flatly. "Because I have your cell phone number—so I could've made that call."

She squeezed her eyes shut for a moment, embarrassed. "And because one of the deputies in town doesn't seem to like you very much."

"Vance? Rick?" Logan sighed heavily. "Believe me, neither one has a valid reason. But right now, I'm concerned about your safety. Do you want Penny and me to come out?"

His calm concern rang true and despite her doubts earlier, she knew in her heart that Logan couldn't be her stalker. What motive could he possibly have?

She went to the windows overlooking the balcony and peered into the calm peaceful night. An owl hooted from a nearby tree. From far away came the faint, distant howl of a coyote, followed by a chorus of the higher pitched yips of its young. But here she could see nothing moving, and a sense of peace settled over her. "No…it's not necessary. I'll let you know if anything else comes up."

TWO

Carrie stood at the open door of her classroom and watched the last child burst out into the hallway.

Marie Colbert, the teacher across the hall, strolled over to join her, her dark curls bouncing with every step. "Why is it," she said with a laugh, "that no matter how much fun we had in class, the kids act like they're escaping a dungeon when they leave? And this is only the first day."

Carrie flicked a glance down the hall, toward the open double doors leading out into the warm Montana sunshine. "I guess lazy summer days are meant for creek stomping, not sitting in class."

Marie cocked her head and studied her. "You look a little tense."

"I'm not sure that turn-of-the-century, American Western art really rang their bells." Carrie shrugged to mask her frustration. "So I talked about how art can be a way to express deep emotions—like that done by refugee children or during wartime, think-ing I might reach the kids who are so addicted to violent video games. But no luck today. I've got a few students who *really* don't want to be here."

Marie smirked. "I'll bet the Nelson twins just *love* all that art."

She'd pinpointed two of Carrie's more challenging students, all right. "How did you know?"

"I had Austin and Dylan when I taught third grade. When they weren't wrestling or lobbing spitballs, they were causing some other kind of ruckus."

"Sounds familiar," Carrie said drily.

"Yeah. It took all year and a trip to the doctor for Ritalin to calm them down." Marie sighed. "I don't think they're taking it anymore, though. I hear they're back to bouncing off the walls in class and haven't learned much ever since."

"It's a tough call for a lot of parents. I don't know what I would do, if it was me." But it wouldn't ever be. After her rocky marriage, she couldn't imagine ever risking another bad choice and that kind of heartbreak again. How could she have been so totally wrong about one of the biggest decisions in life?

She might as well wish for the moon as to long for the happy little family she'd once dreamed of back in her naive, younger days.

"Well, I'd go with the medications that helped them settle down and learn, but that's just me." Marie adjusted her wire-rim glasses. "But, hey, we've already got one day down, and just eight weeks to go. I'll trade you physics for art appreciation any day. You should look at the mess in my room after our gravity experiments this morning."

"Are you a regular teacher here?"

"Honey, I *graduated* from Granite Falls High. I went off to Montana State, came back, and I've taught here ever since. Ten years."

"You must know all of the families well, then."

"It's a really close-knit community. Tourists come and go, but the locals really watch out for each other."

"I'm glad to hear that," Carrie muttered under her breath. *Really glad.*

"Hmm?" Marie gave her a distracted glance as she held up her hand to slow down a straggler racing for the door. "I hear you'll be full-time in the fall. Where did you teach before?"

A brief, painful memory of Billy's erratic, foot-loose ways cut through Carrie's thoughts. "Until now, I've…just been able to do some substituting, now and then. We moved around a lot."

Marie gave her an approving smile. "Lucky you to find a permanent position here. It isn't easy, these days."

"I know. And I'm thankful for this summer job, too. I need the money."

Marie chuckled. "Don't we all. Did you find a decent place to stay?"

"I have to start looking for something long-term in the fall, so let me know if you hear of anything.

I have just a summer lease out at a rafting company property."

"Which one?"

"Wolf River. Logan and Penny Bradley."

"Really." Marie's eyes widened. "How did you end up there?"

"Weeks of searching on the internet—and the first day the apartment was listed, I nabbed it sight unseen. It's really nice," Carrie added, feeling defensive at the hint of incredulity in the other woman's eyes. "Despite being a little noisy with the tourists coming and going on raft trips. I moved in over the weekend, and it was crazy on Sunday."

"I can imagine." Marie looked at her closely. "And what about the Bradleys? Have you had a chance to get to know them?"

"Not really, but they both seem like nice people."

"Yes. Well…I'm sure they are."

The tone in her voice didn't ring quite true. "Is there something I should know?"

After casting a glance down the hall to where several teachers had emerged from their classrooms and were striking up a conversation as they headed toward the door, Marie flashed a diffident smile. "Well, I'm not one to gossip, you know. Maybe I shouldn't say anything."

"Now you have me worried."

"Well…the Bradleys had a little…uh, trouble a year or so ago."

"What kind of trouble?"

"Nothing proven," Marie reassured her. "It all turned out okay…for them. There are people around town who still really want answers, though. Hey, I'd better get busy, or I'll be here all afternoon."

Nothing proven? Uneasy, Carrie watched Marie waggle her fingertips in farewell and scuttle across the hallway to her classroom. First Deputy Munson and now Marie had hinted at trouble, though neither had given her any concrete reason to worry.

So what on earth was going on? Tomorrow afternoon she had to go back to her brother's ranch to pick up the last of her possessions, but when she returned, she was going to find some answers.

Not again. Carrie stilled. Held her breath. There it was—a rustle in the bushes—closer, this time. The muted crunch of pine needles. The snap of a twig.

And another.

It wasn't the bears this time, though she might be the only person who'd ever wished it were. They tore at the garbage can lids with single-minded determination, heedless of the noise they created. But this was too quiet. Too stealthy.

And it wasn't a wolf.

The looming threat out there was human and she'd never felt so alone.

She eased the blinds away from the window and peeked out, thankful that the apartment was darkened already, but frustrated by the dim sliver of moon that had long since slipped behind a threatening blanket of clouds.

Marie's words from this morning ran through her mind again and again. *The Bradleys had experienced a "little" trouble a year or so ago.*

After class ended at noon, Carrie had taken the long trip to Trace's ranch, and hadn't made it back to her apartment until dusk. Logan's pickup was gone, but Penny had just returned with her evening float trip customers and their cars were still parked next to both buildings.

She'd had to park farther away than usual, just beyond the bright pool of light beneath the security lights shining from the peak of the boathouse and the top of a single pole close to the river landing site.

It hadn't seemed important at the time, with a noisy group of rafters chattering along the shore as they peeled off their life jackets. But now...

She drew in a sharp breath as a hunched dark form materialized out of the gloom next to her old SUV and crept from one door to the next, trying the locks. *Lord—what do I do now?*

She could yell and startle him...but what if he then came crashing through her apartment door? Her heart pounding, she stepped away from the window and took a slow, faltering breath, trying to still her trembling fingers and shaking knees as she punched 911 into her cell phone.

Four rings.

Five.

Six.

Why wasn't anyone answering?

Moving back to the edge of the window with the phone at her ear, she furtively stole another look.

The stranger wasn't by her Tahoe. He now stood a few feet away from it, something gleaming at his side. And he was staring right at her window as if he knew exactly where she was standing. As if he were taunting her.

"911. What is your emergency?"

She stood frozen, staring through the blinds as the figure melted back into the shadows.

"You have called 911," the dispatcher said with an edge to his voice. "State your name and the emergency, please."

"I...I think there's someone outside. Trying to break into my SUV."

"Your location?"

"Nine miles north of Granite Falls. Wolf Creek Rafting Company."

"Hold on."

She gripped her phone even tighter as several interminable seconds ticked by. The breeze had picked up, sending branches scraping against the building. The shadows beyond the reach of the security lights seemed to be shifting, coalescing.

Was that someone lurking by the boathouse? At the bumper of her SUV? Or was it just her imagination? Billy had threatened to make trouble—was it him?

From some distant place in the darkness she heard the faint sound of a distant engine roaring to life... then fade, heading toward the highway.

"Ma'am, I have an officer who should be there within twenty minutes. Are you alone?"

"Yes." *More than I've ever been in my life.*

"Stay inside. Keep your doors and windows locked."

He certainly had a knack for stating the obvious. "Believe me, I will," she said wryly. "But I...I think I heard a car start up. Maybe he left it hidden somewhere up the lane and now he's gone."

"Do you still want the officer to stop out?"

"No..." She bit her lip. "On second thought, please. If this guy is still in the area and sees a patrol car arrive, it might scare him off."

"Yes, ma'am. The officer will get there as soon as he can."

Carrie leaned her head against the window frame and peered through the edge of the blinds. The parking lot was empty. Only the sounds of the river and the breeze-tossed branches filled the silence.

But this incident brought back memories of other nights last fall, when she'd tried to still her racing heart. When a threatening phone call or email had kept her on edge. When Billy had promised to make her pay.

And there'd been another one of his cryptic emails

just last night. A subtle threat. A promise that when he came back to Montana, he was planning on a little visit.

The figure out in the darkness *had* seemed a little…taller than him, though that could have been a trick of the lighting, or a perception enhanced by her own fear.

But what if he was back in Montana and had already found her?

Counting the slow drag of the minutes on her watch, Carrie shivered in the chilly night air, unable to tear herself away from the window. What if the stranger came back? What if he managed to quietly pick the lock on her door?

Harley padded across the room to wind around her ankles like a warm, sinuous powder puff, then stalked away and curled up on the back of the sofa where he promptly went to sleep.

"Some watch cat *you* are," she muttered.

The most interest he'd shown since their arrival Sunday had been over the appearance of Logan's golden lab. The cat had patrolled the windowsills for ten minutes after the sighting, the low grumble in his throat promising no quarter if he ever got the chance to attack.

The dog didn't appear very energetic. It had apparently slept away the afternoon in the boathouse, and had only emerged to jump into Logan's truck when he got ready to leave yesterday evening. With all the people around, it hadn't uttered a single bark.

But still, a dog *might* offer a sense of security, and her brother's fiancée, Kris, did run an animal shelter...though it would be a long drive to check out the possibilities for a good, noisy companion.

"I wonder if Logan would like to make a temporary trade?" She studied her sleeping cat, who opened one eye, offered a bored yawn and went back to sleep. "Maybe not."

At the crunch of tires on gravel she stiffened, a hand at her throat...then relaxed when a patrol car marked with K-9 Patrol on the side pulled to a stop.

Relief flooded through her when a deputy stepped out with a clipboard in hand. He wasn't the rumpled, overweight teddy bear of an officer she'd met in town, though. This one was thin, austere-looking and older, his uniform crisply pressed, his military-cut, salt-and-pepper hair silvered by security light overhead.

She stepped out of her apartment onto the balcony. "I'm so glad you're here," she called out as she descended the stairs and crossed the parking area to meet him.

"Deputy Rick Peterson." He accepted her handshake. "I hear you've had a little trouble?"

"There was someone out here, trying to break into my Tahoe. I keep it locked, so he couldn't get in. I know it's probably not a big deal, but I'm here alone." The police dog in the backseat of the patrol started barking. "Maybe your buddy has picked up his scent, or something."

"Had any trouble out here before?"

"I just moved in Sunday afternoon and thought I had a prowler last night, as well. This is the first I've actually seen him."

"You surely haven't had enough time to make any enemies here." He looked at her over his half-rim glasses. "Or have you?"

She shook her head. "No. But one might've followed me from the past."

He pursed his lips as she told him about Billy, then he flicked on his flashlight and circled her vehicle. She followed on his heels and peered inside, too.

"Are you missing anything?"

Her boxes of books were still on the backseat, along with her old camera bag and an even older ink-jet printer. "Everything is still there—not that anyone could want it." She tried the door handles. "And the car is still locked. I suppose I've called you on a wild-goose chase."

"Not a problem. If a stranger was out here lurking around, I can understand why you'd be concerned." He scanned the wide parking area and beyond that, the dark, nearly impenetrable pine forest that rimmed the clearing on three sides. "Maybe you'd be better off finding a place in town. Closer to civilization."

"I tried, but no dice. I'll have to find a different place by September, though."

"Our county sheriff's department is understaffed and we have a lot of ground to cover. If you do encounter trouble out here, we might not be able to respond as fast as we'd like."

She nodded, biting her lower lip. "I understand. I still hope my past isn't going to be an issue. But I'll let the Bradleys know about it."

His eyebrows drew together. "Still, a lady living alone like you might want to take a gun safety course and keep a weapon around. There's other varmints out here besides the two-legged kind."

"I grew up on a ranch. I've had my own shotgun since I was twelve."

"Is it here?"

"It's in the back of my SUV."

He snorted. "Won't do you much good in there."

"I didn't want to bring it in until I had time to install a padlock on my closet. There are families with kids all over this property during the day. If one came upstairs and found it while I wasn't home…" She shuddered.

He went to the back door of the SUV. "Ma'am, I recommend that you take it upstairs for the rest of the night. Just firing off a warning shot might do a world of good if that prowler comes back. It could take us a long time to get here."

She could only imagine the deputy's amusement

if he saw her battered 1960s Remington shotgun, a gift from her grandfather.

Years ago, back when she was a teenager, she'd left one of the ranch dogs in her pickup cab while she'd struggled to catch and treat a calf with scours, and the dog had chewed the butt of the wooden stock to splinters. The weapon was old but accurate, and sentiment had kept her from trading it off.

She patted her pockets. "I...don't have my keys on me."

He tipped his head toward the front door. "Looks like you have a keypad, though."

She pulled a face. "It doesn't work. I can just take care of this tomorrow."

His gaze sharpened. "Go ahead and get your keys. I don't mind waiting."

At the hint of suspicion in his voice she sighed, and dutifully ran upstairs to retrieve her keys from the kitchen table. If he'd misread her hesitation and thought he was going to make headlines by finding stolen loot or a few hundred pounds of pot in her trunk, he was going to be sadly disappointed.

She unlocked the liftgate, opened it and stepped aside while it lifted on its own.

His eyes flared wide when he saw the only contents—the old shotgun and a box of shells. "That's... it? Does it even work?"

"It actually shoots true, even if it looks a little rough." The barking from inside the patrol car grew more frantic. "Does your dog need to be let out, or something?"

"I just started my shift. He shouldn't."

Now, Carrie could hear the sound of its claws scrabbling against the windows. "I'm glad you aren't letting him loose. He sounds fierce."

"Ranger's new to the department, and he's still erratic." The deputy scowled toward his vehicle, a thoughtful look spreading across his face. "But he does know his business. Maybe—"

The radio mike at his shoulder crackled with static. A rapid-fire dispatcher's voice rattled off a series of codes, then an address.

Peterson listened, tapped a button on the mike and muttered a response as he strode to his vehicle and pulled open the front door.

He paused, half-inside, and looked back. "Accident on the highway. I have to leave. But don't hesitate to call the dispatcher if you have any problems. Believe me, we'd rather answer a false alarm now and then, than have to deal with the aftermath if someone fails to call in time."

THREE

The clerk, a stocky middle-aged woman with Norma emblazoned on her name badge, finished ringing up Carrie's last item. "You must be planning on a blizzard in June, with all these groceries."

Carrie smiled at the teenage boy bagging the last of her purchases and rescued a bottle of Diet Coke before it disappeared into a bag with her canned goods. "With a weekend ahead, I probably won't want to brave the tourist traffic to come back into town."

"And this is just mid-June. Wait till the Fourth of July." Chewing on her lower lip, Norma tilted her head and studied the name on Carrie's check, then slid it into the cash register and handed her the receipt. "There was someone in here asking about you the other day."

Small-town gossips at work, no doubt. Carrie rolled her eyes. "I hope you had good things to say."

"It was some guy who wondered if I knew where you lived."

Carrie stilled. "He? Did he say who he was?"

Norma thought for a moment. "Nope. It was real busy at the time. He didn't buy anything, just sort of cut into the line to ask me and then he left."

"Do you remember what he looked like?"

"I just had a glimpse of him, but he was a nice-looking man. Dark hair. Thirties, maybe."

Which could be Billy or a thousand other guys. But how many other guys would be looking for *her?* Carrie fidgeted with her key ring. "Do you remember what day?"

"Honey, at my age the days sort of blur together. It was early in the week, anyways. I know I haven't seen you since then."

"Did you tell him where I live?"

"I may be getting old, but I'm not stupid. If he was an axe murderer, I'd never forgive myself. But," Norma added, "everyone in town knows about you being the new teacher here. And with the Bradleys' trouble last year and you staying out there, word gets around."

Which meant there was a good chance someone might have shared that information without a second thought. But then again, maybe the guy had been totally innocent. Someone needing to deliver a package, perhaps.

But Norma would've noticed a FedEx or UPS uniform.

Carrie managed a smile. "Thanks for letting me know."

Norma's forehead creased into a worried frown. "Maybe I shouldn't have said anything. You look worried."

"Believe me, I want to know."

Norma gave her head a decisive nod. "Well, if I see this fella again, I'll be sure to tell you. And he won't be getting any information from me."

Carrie smiled in thanks as she headed for the exit, the bag boy following at her heels with the cart. *Small towns,* she thought with an inward sigh. Friendly, connected and sometimes entirely too trusting. Maybe Norma would be careful…but what if it was already too late?

The view was perfect, from the shaded spot between the drugstore and Marv's Saddle Shop and Shoe Repair. The tourists window-shopping along Main Street were a better cover yet. And if anyone else saw him, it wouldn't matter. He blended right into the fabric of this vacation destination town.

He watched with satisfaction when Carrie stepped out of the grocery store. She paused, shaded her eyes with her hand, and scanned both sides of the street as if she *knew* someone was watching.

He remained motionless, his dull clothes fading into the shadows and the dark gray wall behind him, his hat settled low over his eyes. She'd come so close to seeing him, several times, it was almost funny. Now, her gaze flitted past him. Hesitated. Then swept by him once more before moving on.

It was amusing to observe her inability to protect herself, to clearly identify danger, even in this innocuous setting.

He smiled to himself. He had time. He'd nose around, and find out exactly what was going on out at the Wolf River Rafting Company. And when he was ready, he'd pay her a little visit so she'd receive a taste of what was to come.

He could hardly wait.

It felt so good—so *normal*—to walk into her classroom the next morning, that Carrie smiled to herself. She hadn't slept well at all last night, with the grocery clerk's words running through her thoughts in an endless litany and her ears attuned to the slightest sounds outside. That stranger hadn't just been casually looking for her around town. He'd wanted to find out where she *lived*. Had someone blithely shared the information—and sent that prowler to her door?

Since Monday night she'd felt restless during the day, too. Wary. Repeatedly had a crawling sensation at the back of her neck at odd times and would whirl around, only to find that nobody was there. But here at school, surrounded by all of the kids and teachers, she could finally relax.

Just ten feet inside the door of her classroom, Carrie saw a creased piece of paper on her desk.

Ordinary typing paper. Nothing unusual. Except that even from a distance, the carnage drawn on it sent a flutter of distaste through her midsection and unsettled the peanut butter and marmalade toast she'd eaten on the way into town.

Some fifth-grade boys liked to doodle in the margins of their notebooks…weapons and bombs and war scenes. That was nothing new. But as she drew closer, the exquisite detail and blatant suffering in the characters' eyes were too real, and an entirely different slant from the norm.

One monstrous, semihuman figure had a look of pure evil on its face, with oversize sharp teeth, and was bedecked with multiple guns and swords and knives. Several bodies lay dismembered on the rough ground, blood flowing from them to mingle and form a river of crimson that ran to the edge of the page.

She shuddered as she stared down at it, an uneasy feeling forming in the pit of her stomach.

It was fifth-grade-level art, in style and execution, but the artist must have spent *hours* on the fine detail. Granted, this was a humanities enrichment class focusing on art appreciation. Maybe the child had been proud of his work and wanted to share it. She leaned closer, then turned the paper over.

But if so, why hadn't he—or she—signed it?

"What's up?"

At the unexpected voice behind her, Carrie startled and spun around, a hand at her throat.

Marie grinned. "Sorry—I thought you heard me say hello from the doorway."

"I didn't. I was studying a picture left on my desk." Carrie handed her the drawing. "Creepy, isn't it?"

Marie gave it a superficial glance and rolled her eyes. "Boys."

"I know. But this is more than that. Look at the faces, and amazing detail. There aren't just *X*'s for the eyes of the dead. These people are *hurting*."

"Yeah, well…you're the art teacher. This was probably done by some kid who's a little more advanced. So, would you like to meet for lunch this afternoon?"

Advanced in artistic skills, true…but also possibly troubled. Carrie dropped her gaze to the drawing once more. Just holding it gave her a sense of the child's intense emotions. *Please, God, don't let this mean that this child is suffering through a bad situation.*

She closed her eyes, visualizing each of the twelve students in her class. All of the boys wore T-shirts and shorts or faded jeans; most of the girls wore pretty summer tops. Had she seen any bruises? Unusual behavior? Nothing that she could recall.

"Uh…Carrie?"

"Sorry. Yes—lunch sounds wonderful." She slid the drawing into the top drawer of her desk and dropped her purse into the bottom drawer. "Any place you choose."

"Silver Bear Café, south edge of town. Best place in town, and the tourists haven't found it yet. There'd be a half-hour wait at any of the touristy places. By the way," she added with a lift of an eyebrow, "I hear you had some excitement on Monday night."

Carrie's heart sank. "News sure traveled fast."

"Courtesy of my police scanner." Marie chuckled. "Everyone has one around here—it's faster than just heading down to the feed store or café to hear the latest news. Memorize all those official code numbers, and it's a *wealth* of information."

"Great. So now the whole county knows the new schoolteacher makes unnecessary 911 calls, and is apparently afraid of the dark?"

"Just because there wasn't a prowler still out there when Rick showed up doesn't mean you didn't have one."

At the ruckus emanating from the riverbank, Logan set aside his camera, took a last disgusted look at the massive rip he'd just photographed as evidence for the insurance company—too straight and even to have been from natural causes—along the deflated, fifteen-foot side tube of one of the larger rubber rafts, and strolled over to check out the latest fishing disaster.

Sure enough, the Nelson twins were in the thick of things—teasing and chortling over the tangled lines of two younger boys. Another two ignored the others as they sat on the bank tossing rocks into the water.

"Dylan, Austin, lay off," Logan said mildly as he took hold of the fistful of tightly knotted filament. It was too tangled to ever pull apart. He eyed the two younger boys, both with nearly white-blond hair, who had come out just a couple times with the older ones. "Looks like you tried to get this apart, and it just got worse. Right?"

The boys nodded.

"Some days are just like that. Let's see. You are… Robbie and Danny?"

They both nodded.

"Fifth grade?" Logan guessed high, hoping to elicit a smile.

"Third." Danny's lower lip trembled. "Robbie's in fourth."

"Do your parents know you're out here?"

"We rode our bikes," Danny said evasively, dropping his gaze to the rocky ground.

"Mom has to work on Saturdays. She don't care," Robbie added with a defiant tilt to his chin. "Just so we get back for supper, is all."

"I see." Logan pulled a knife from the sheath at his belt and cut away the mass of fishing line, then reattached each hook and bobber. "There you go, boys. What did you say your last name was?"

"Jensen," Danny piped up as he eagerly reached for his rod.

"Now he's gonna tell, stupid," Robbie hissed,

elbowing his younger brother in the ribs. "See if we get to go fishing then."

"I don't care if you're here, but your mom does need to know and give her permission. Okay? The river can be a dangerous place."

"Nobody owns the river," Robbie shot back. "We learned that in school."

"You're right," Logan countered, hiding a smile at the boy's spunk. "But the land is mine, and since I'm the responsible adult here, I just want you to be safe. *And* for your mom to say it's okay."

"But…but this is the best spot on the whole river. Clear back to town."

"I know. It slows down along this stretch, and there are nice deep trout pools close to the bank. There's a good one just a dozen yards down from the raft launching area."

Robbie's brow furrowed with intense concentration. "Can we come again if we bring a note?"

"That would be good, though I also need to tell her that I can't be responsible for you. All of the other moms had to do the same thing—talk to me, and write a note, if their boys wanted to be here."

Robbie and Danny looked at each other.

"Phone number?" Logan prodded gently. He punched the numbers into his cell phone as the older boy recited them, then hit Send.

It didn't take long to discover why the boys both looked so crestfallen. After he explained the situation, there was a brief silence, then the decibel level of their mother's voice rose with each word, until he had to hold the phone well away from his ear. She disconnected before he could say a single word in the boys' defense.

"Sorry, guys. She says you can't be riding your bikes down the highway, and you are not allowed near the river." He smiled at them, trying to soften the news, though the quiet snickers of the Nelson twins from a few yards away didn't help matters.

Danny's eyes glistened with tears, but Robbie's face reddened. *"Never?"*

"She says you can't come here alone. But maybe when you're older, okay?"

"Are we grounded?" Danny whispered, a tear trailing down his cheek.

For a lifetime and a half, if his mother's voice was any clue.

Logan ruffled the boy's hair, wishing he dared give him a hug. Knowing it would be improper and even dangerous to offer that comfort. "She didn't tell me. She only said that she'd be here in fifteen minutes to take you both home. Do you have a dog?"

"Mom doesn't like dogs. They're messy," Robbie muttered.

"Want to see mine?" Logan held two fingers to his mouth and sent off a piercing whistle. A few seconds later, Murphy appeared at the door of the boathouse, blinked at the sunshine, then ambled over to sit at Logan's feet.

"He's just a lazy ole dog," Robbie said.

"You think? Take a look." Logan silently signaled and Murphy rolled over. "Ask him a simple math question. Kindergarten level."

A smile glimmered on Danny's face. "One plus two?"

Murphy waved his tail furiously, and with each of his three deep barks, the child's smile grew. *"Wow."*

Even Robbie was showing more interest now. "What else can he do?"

"Do you have a good arm for throwing?"

"Yeah."

Logan searched the ground, picked up an old yellow tennis ball and lobbed it into a high, long-distance arc. The old lab tore across parking lot and was there to catch it as it fell.

Now all the boys were watching. One of the Nelson twins tried to intercept the dog when it returned, but it neatly circumvented him and stopped at Logan's feet. Logan handed the ball to Robbie. "Give it a try. And don't worry about throwing as high as I did—grounders are good, too. He'll do this until he gets too tired."

True to form, Murphy chased after the ball for Robbie several times, and then Danny, until both boys were grinning and cheering Murphy on.

"Nice job," Carrie said quietly. "You handled that very well."

Logan turned and found her perched on the top of a picnic table in front of the boathouse. He reined in his automatic flash of pleasure at seeing her there. "I didn't know you were out here."

"You were occupied. Very well, by the way. You could've been a great teacher. Or a counselor."

"Thanks. I once thought about teaching at a university—livestock production or horse management, maybe. But…well, things changed at home and my sister and I both headed back to the family ranch after we graduated from college."

"So where is home?"

"An hour or so from here." He hitched his shoulder a little, brushing aside the raw memories of struggling to save the ranch. "My mother won a fierce battle with cancer, but my dad ended up having to sell out to pay off her medical bills."

"I'm so sorry."

"Don't be. She's in remission, and my dad would've given the earth to make her well."

"Where are they now?"

"Florida. She'd always dreamed of retiring there but never thought it possible. Now Dad manages a quarter horse breeding farm south of Tampa, and Mom has a part-time job in a gift shop. They say it's like living a second honeymoon every single day."

She smiled at that. "Sounds like a happy marriage."

"It is." He angled a rueful look at her. "Kinda hard to follow an act like that. They still hold hands at sixty."

"So you're one of those guys looking for perfection?" she teased.

"I'm just not looking," he shot back, softening his words with a quick grin. But it was the truth. He'd stored away his wounded heart long ago, after Janie died, and he had no intention of getting into any conversations about it. How had they gotten onto *this* topic?

He shifted uneasily, thankful to hear the sound of a vehicle coming up the lane. As it came into view, he could see Montana plates—and from the duet of groans from the two boys, knew it probably belonged to their mother.

The SUV pulled to a hard stop, and a slender woman stepped out, her jaw rigid. "Boys—get your bikes over here right now. We'll put them in the back."

With a faint nod in Logan's direction, she marched to the rear, lifted the tailgate, and helped the boys load the bikes. Their eyes were downcast as they climbed in, though Danny braved a quick, longing glance toward Murphy before he pulled his door shut and slumped into his seat.

Their mother paused at her own door, clearly unhappy and torn between a swift getaway and common manners. The manners won when she finally looked up at Logan for a split second before her gaze darted away. "The boys will not bother you again."

"They weren't a bother. I just want parents to

know when their kids are out here. I can't be responsible for them while I'm working, and that river current is dangerous."

"As I said, they won't be back." She slid into her seat, hesitated, then her gaze locked on his. "Sheryl Colwell was a friend of mine. I'm sure you understand."

The SUV left in a cloud of dust.

The other kids had wandered back to their fishing poles as soon as Murphy tired of fetching and plopped down under a tree.

Now Logan could feel Carrie's curious gaze on his back. He could sense that she was turning the woman's words over in her mind, wondering what it all meant.

Unless she knew already, in which case this just confirmed whatever gossip she'd heard in town.

"When I walked over here, I saw you studying the raft. What's going on?"

Surprised at the change of topic, he looked over his shoulder. "Damage. Tina and Penny don't remember hitting any sharp boulders on the river during the evening float trip yesterday. They couldn't have reached the landing site downriver unless it happened during the last few minutes anyway. And when they hauled the raft back here, it was still fully inflated."

"So it happened here. On the shore."

"Vandalism."

She moved closer to the raft and bent down to

inspect it. She reached out to touch the damaged area and her hand brushed against his.

She jerked her hand back as if she'd touched fire, a flash of confusion crossing her face, and he knew she'd felt it, too—an electric sensation that had shot up his arm and landed somewhere in the vicinity of his heart.

"Um…" She blinked. "A knife, maybe?"

"That's my guess."

Frowning, she straightened and shaded her eyes with her hand as she studied the boys along the riverbank. "Think it was any of those kids?"

"The four here now all come from the Sundown Trailer Court—and that's not the trailer park with the fancy security fences and beautiful landscaping. Sundown is shabby, with beer bottles and trash thrown around. It doesn't sound like the boys get much parenting, so they're probably just glad to have a free place to hang out."

"Still…"

"Nope. They hang around quite a bit, and they're all good kids. Now, anyways," he added with a grin. "We had to discuss manners a few times early on."

Carrie bit her lower lip, her eyes troubled. "If not them, then who? Why would anyone want to cause you trouble?"

"Believe me, this wasn't the first time something happened here during the past year. And it probably won't be the last."

She appeared to be oddly relieved at the news. "I thought the prowler on Monday night was stalking me, but maybe not."

"Stalking you?"

"I know, it probably sounds silly. But my ex-husband, Billy, wasn't all that happy about our divorce, even though he initiated it. I get threatening calls from him now and then."

Logan frowned. "Worrying about something like that doesn't sound silly at all."

"But he couldn't know where I am right now." She flipped a hand dismissively. "I made sure of that when I left my brother's ranch."

"Still…"

"So, do you think that prowler was the one who damaged your raft?"

"Nope." He ran a hand over the damaged surface. "We would've noticed yesterday when we tried to put it on the river. But it was fine."

"What if he was just scoping things out, and came back last night?"

"Maybe."

She pulled a cell phone from the pocket of her khaki slacks and offered it to him. "You should call the sheriff's department."

He sighed, thinking of the other suspicious events on the rafting company property and his cabin over the past twelve months. "I don't think so."

"Why not? You'll need a police report to file an insurance claim, right?"

He laughed at that. "I took photos, but my insurance company has become a little testy when I call."

"But that's their *job*. Answering your calls. Taking care of your claims."

"Within reason."

"Well, if I were you—" Her eyes widened with sudden understanding. "This isn't the first time you've had trouble."

"No, ma'am."

"But…why?" Her gaze swept the dense forest of pines crowding in on three sides of the clearing. "And why doesn't the sheriff's department help?"

He thought about all the ways they'd failed to properly investigate. The morning after someone shot out a window in his cabin. Or the day he'd found his tires slashed. Or the other, more subtle events that illustrated exactly what local opinion was regarding his character.

Given the offhand attitude and smirk on the face of the deputy who'd responded to his calls, any amount of trouble at Wolf River Rafting Company was what Logan deserved, and more.

"I'm sure they're busy enough as it is," he said finally. "And what are they going to do? A little vandalism won't warrant some big investigation."

"I think there's more to all of this than just that." She regarded him for a long moment. "Since I moved to town, two deputies and a teacher have hinted that I should be worried about living here. I ignored them, because I think you and your sister seem like nice people. But now Robbie and Danny's mom acted like she didn't want them to ever come out here, no matter what. So what's going on?"

No wonder she hadn't packed her bags and fled to town after her first day here. She didn't know.

"Well?"

He felt the old, familiar weight of sadness and regrets crush his heart. "Probably because everyone in the county, barring a few jurors, still believes I murdered Sheryl Colwell."

FOUR

"**W**-who was Sheryl Colwell?" Carrie stared at Logan, still not believing what he'd just said. *Murder?*

That he'd been tried in a court of law meant there had been evidence. Good evidence. And that the sheriff's department and district attorney had been convinced of his guilt. From the oblique warnings she'd received, at least two deputies still believed he was a dangerous man. Had she been living this close to a cold-blooded killer? Chatting casually with a man capable of violence?

And he knew exactly how alone she was out here, on these long, cold Montana nights.

Logan's expression turned stoic, as if he knew she was judging him and had already found him guilty. "Sheryl was a nice lady, far as I know. Thirty-two, with a husband and son."

She drew in a sharp breath. "Is her son Noah Colwell?"

"That's right."

"I've had him in class a whole week and didn't know anything about it. Poor boy—I have yet to hear him say a word in class. I just thought he was shy." She felt her heart squeeze at the thought of all Noah had been through. "No wonder he's so withdrawn."

"His father has been intensely protective of the kid ever since. His sister came to live with them, since he has to travel quite a bit. He's sometimes gone for weeks at a time."

"That's *awful*."

Logan stared off at some distant point on the horizon, his voice flat and emotionless. "It was all part of the prosecution's summation—how an innocent young child lost his mother due to one heinous act of violence, and has an even more disrupted family life because of his dad's absences as a long-haul trucker. The attorney made it clear just how traumatized the boy was—to the point that he had barely spoken after his mom's death. And maybe that was all true. But someone else killed her."

She searched his face, trying to find the truth in his words. Wondering what she should believe. "If you were acquitted, why would those deputies still think you're guilty?"

"Frankly, I don't know why they ever thought so in the first place."

The logical, practical side of her urged her to grab her keys and flee to the safety of Granite Falls. A growing feeling in her heart told her that this man couldn't possibly be guilty of such a terrible crime. "But it's over now, right?"

"Not at all." He wearily shook his head. "I think the sheriff figured it was an easy, high-profile case, and expected it to wrap up with a nice, tidy conviction just before reelection time. Instead, my lawyer proved reasonable doubt and made him and his department appear inept. Which was true."

"And the locals…"

"Some still figure this was just one more case where a crooked lawyer managed to set a killer free. Small-town gossip just doesn't die."

"I know. I grew up near a small town like this one, and memories run deep. As in, 'Jane Doe? Oh, yeah—she's the one whose mother had the affair with that doctor over in Evansville back in 1982.'" Carrie faltered to a stop as heat started creeping up the back of her neck. *Way to go…now you're babbling.* "Uh, well…some things just brand you for life in a small town."

As if he didn't already know that from recent, bitter experience—a fact that he'd made perfectly clear. Even more embarrassed, she clamped her mouth shut.

He met her gaze squarely, as if he'd just read her thoughts, a muscle ticking along the side of his jaw. "If you want to tear up your lease contract, I'll refund the deposit. But if you have any questions that could help set your mind at ease, fire away."

"How well did you know Sheryl?"

"We ran into each other on Main Street now and then, and she came out for a couple of float trips. Once with her boy, then she came again alone. That's it. End of story. We were just casual acquaintances. And on both raft trips there was a full load of passengers—tourists from all over the country, so neither trip included the intimate interlude that the prosecutor implied."

"You were the guide?"

"Just by chance, both times. Tina hadn't finished her training and safety certification yet."

"So…what was Sheryl like?"

"As I said, she was a nice lady. Quiet. I don't think she asked a single question during either trip. In fact, she seemed a little scared of the water. And when we beached the raft at our midway point for a riverside lunch, the other passengers took a hike up to Badger Peak rather than take time to eat. She was the only one who stayed behind, and she read a book the whole time. Said she didn't like heights."

"I suppose the other passengers were questioned, and said you two had…plenty of time alone together."

"Right. The prosecutor tried to prove it was the start of an ongoing affair, if that's what you're getting at it." Logan snorted. "So given the supposed affair, she later committed suicide? Or I killed her in a jealous rage because she wouldn't leave her husband? None of that makes sense."

"And if there was no proof—"

"Oh, there was 'proof' all right. An imprint of a Chaco sandal near where she fell off the cliff. In my size…as if most outdoors enthusiasts around here don't wear that kind of sandal."

"That's it?"

"A scout troop saw me in the area earlier, while they were out working on a hiking badge." He heaved a sigh. "I was out hiking myself. And since I was up in the mountains alone most of the day, I had no alibi for the hours in question. A witness claimed Sheryl said she'd been seeing me on the sly. There was more, but none of it was true."

Carrie had watched enough old *Law & Order* reruns to know that some serial killers possessed enough charm to gain their victims' confidence. But if Logan was lying about this, he was incredibly good at it. Even with her gaze riveted on his face she hadn't seen so much as a flicker of guilt or deceit.

"I guess…I just don't know what to say," she said finally.

"All I know is that I'm innocent, and that I'm not going to stop searching until I find the guy who did kill her." A corner of his mouth lifted wryly. "Though there's a saying about how there are no guilty prisoners on death row, so I guess you'll have to decide for yourself just what you want to believe."

* * *

Before talking to Logan on Saturday, Carrie would've automatically believed the sheriff's department over a claim of innocence by a man she barely knew.

Yet she'd already seen Logan's gentleness with the local kids and his teasing banter with Penny. His wry, self-deprecating humor and quiet sense of honor. She'd been drawn to him for those very reasons, and that feeling had grown with every passing day.

Those *surely* couldn't be traits of a killer.

All day Sunday she'd been able to think of nothing else. Wavering from one hour to the next as to whether or not she'd be wise to just leave. Praying for guidance.

And then, in the evening, she'd happened to look down from her apartment window to find Logan sitting on the open tailgate of the company pickup with his head bowed, one arm draped around the dog sitting at his side. Penny was there, too, her hand on his shoulder and her own head bowed.

Carrie had no delusions about the fact that even the worst of sinners might pray for forgiveness. And should. Yet the closeness of that scene, and the obvious love Penny had for her brother, touched Carrie's heart in a way all of the logical thinking in the world had not.

If Logan had been shunned by this town for something he hadn't done, how could she do the same?

She jerked her attention back to her classroom, hit the off button on the TV remote, and popped the DVD out of the player. It was her favorite—a depiction of the American cowboy as portrayed in paintings and sculpture by Remington.

"So," she said with a smile, "how did Remington's subjects differ from the ranches and cowboys we see today?"

Seven pairs of eyes stared blankly at her, quiet and obedient, while in one corner of the room, Noah Colwell silently stared down at the top of his desk, his thin shoulders hunched. In the other back corner, the Nelson twins looked at each other and rolled their eyes.

"Austin?"

That earned a guilty glance from the twin who seemed quieter, and snickers from his brother— who was her most likely candidate as creator of the violent drawings left on her desk on Monday, and again today.

"Dylan?"

His snickers died as Dylan silently lifted his chin in subtle defiance.

"Does anyone here live on a ranch?" She scanned the room. Two girls raised tentative hands. There were at least four others, out of the twelve students in her class, but no one else volunteered a hand. "Well, I'll bet *all* of you have seen ranchers and cowhands come into town. Are their hats just the same now as they were back in the days of the Wild West? How about their chaps, and their saddles?"

The students seemed to collectively slide down in their chairs and avoid meeting her eyes. Not unexpected, she realized with an inward smile. Middle school was such a tender time for being easily mortified by unwanted attention or, worse, saying something that might make classmates scoff.

"Well, our next project will be creating either a watercolor or acrylic painting in the style of Remington, but with the cowboys wearing modern-day apparel and using present-day equipment. So think hard on it overnight, and we'll see you here tomorrow." All twelve students scrambled to their feet and bolted for freedom.

One, a beautiful Latina with shimmering hair that swung down her back to her waist, hesitated when she reached the door. "I won't be in class the rest of the week," she said with a shy duck of her head. "Can I do a makeup assignment for anything I miss?"

"No problem, Isabella. We can talk about it when you get back."

The girl flashed a smile and joined the melee of students in the hallway.

Marie Colbert made her way through the crowd to join Carrie. "Is it only Monday? I, for one, need to find a place to put my feet up for a while."

"More experiments?"

"Every day." She blew at the bangs drooping over

one eye. "I need to keep the scalawags occupied or there'll be an uprising. How about you?"

Carrie glanced over her shoulder toward her own classroom. "Do you have a minute?"

Marie shrugged and followed her inside. "What's up?"

"Hold on." Carrie walked the perimeter of the room, scanning the counters, bookshelves and desktops, her heart lifting with relief. *All clear.*

But at her desk, she sighed and reached for an unfamiliar sheet of paper that had apparently been left facedown on one corner while her back was turned. "Another. I'd hoped there wouldn't be."

"Another what?" Marie joined her, craning her neck to see the paper Carrie held in her hands.

"I got distracted by Isabella's question and I didn't see who left this, but this makes three of these pictures so far. Two of them today. I have yet to figure out who the artist is."

Marie gave her a curious look. "It *still* looks like the usual boy stuff, to me. Weapons. Mayhem. Explosions."

"Right. But look closer at the nightmarish quality. The *suffering.* Just like the first one I showed you."

Carrie handed her the picture and leaned over to retrieve a manila folder from her top left desk drawer. She opened it and spread the other two drawings out on her desk. "The child still leaves them secretly, so I won't know who it is."

"Strange gifts," Marie admitted.

"They aren't gifts. Not really. I'm afraid they're a message—like a call for help, or something."

Marie rolled her eyes. "And I think you might be the one with the overactive imagination. Believe me—I see this kind of stuff doodled on assignments all the time."

"I have, too. But look at all these slashing lines and the detail. And why are they being left anonymously for a teacher? I'm worried that they're either from a child who's living in a violent situation, or even a child filled with a lot of rage."

Marie pursed her lips. "I don't know if I'd go *that* far."

"Why would a child spend so much time on them and then leave them for me to find, if it wasn't some sort of message? I know young boys like to draw stuff like this. But not to this extent."

"Maybe this kid is just proud of his drawings and wants recognition."

"If that was the case, he'd sign them."

"Unless he's a little shy. Maybe he's waiting to see a positive reaction before coming forward."

Carrie suppressed a shudder. "I don't think that's it."

"I'd forget about it, if I were you." Marie patted Carrie's hand. "Toss them all and forget about it."

"Maybe Principal Grover—"

"Just drop it. I know the kids in your class. Some come from broken homes. A few have had some troubles, and a few tend to cause it. But there's nothing to get all ruffled over and I'm sure Ed would say the same thing." Marie's voice lowered. "And honestly, he gets impatient with inexperienced teachers because he'd rather not be bothered with all of this inconsequential stuff."

Inconsequential? Carrie bit back a sharp reply. "I think I need to start going through some of their school files, and wonder if you can give me some ideas on where to start. Noah seems like my best bet. What do you think?"

"Just because he lost his mom? No...he was a very quiet child before her death, and he's got a very protective dad and an aunt who moved into the family home to give him more stability." She fiddled with the ring of keys in her hand. "They've had him in counseling ever since, or so I've heard... so he should have a lot of support. Anyway, I can't see a shy boy like him getting into all of this...this artistic carnage."

"The Nelson twins, then? And Ashley has a surly attitude like no other. Maybe I'm wrong, but the others just don't seem like possibilities."

Marie's mouth flattened. "Look, hon. I'm trying to tell you something here. This isn't a big deal. And we're teaching 'summer enrichment,' not part of the formal school calendar. Far as I'm concerned, we're providing free child care and entertainment for the summer."

"But—"

"Normal kid stuff. Nothing more." Marie waggled her fingertips as she headed for the door. "Just a word to the wise, as they say—especially since you're new on board. When it comes time for contract renewals every spring, well…squeaky wheels sometimes end up rolling right out of town."

"Squeaky wheels. Was that why there was an opening for a teacher here? Someone else cared enough to buck the system in some way and found herself packing?"

Marie turned back at the doorway and glared at her. "Whoa. You aren't the only one who cares about these kids, and you're taking this way too far."

"I…I'm sorry. Of course you care. I didn't mean to slam everyone here." Carrie bit her lower lip. "But I just have to wonder if this is one way that school violence takes place—when no one bothers to watch out for the troubled kids who need help?"

"If that were the case here, but it's not. When you get a few years under your belt, you'll have a more balanced view, believe me." Marie held a hand up and fluttered her fingertips and she left the room.

Gripping the edge of her desk with both hands, Carrie watched her leave, and then she dropped her gaze to the pictures. Marie was wrong.

In two of the pictures, bare tree limbs clawed at a turbulent sky, rising from a dead tree. A raging, crimson river—*of blood?*—slammed against its rocky banks and shot over massive boulders in its path. There seemed to be some sort of war scene on the other side, with people fighting with cannon and swords and guns, and mutilated bodies strewn on the ground.

Someone had taken *hours* to achieve this degree of detail, and she'd stake her teaching certificate on the fact that he was a troubled child reaching out for help.

She closed her eyes and reviewed those last few moments of the class period when the students had charged for the door, and tried to picture who might be the most likely suspects.

Marie hadn't appeared concerned about anyone in the class, but the Nelson twins were certainly a rambunctious pair. The wicked gleam in Dylan's eyes promised trouble and she could easily guess that his more timid brother was probably on board with whatever Dylan dreamed up. Their mother didn't exactly look like the other parents who waited in cars outside the school, either, with her Gabby's Tavern T-shirts, frowsy blond hair and the tattoos crawling up both arms. To have that same T-shirt in several colors probably meant she waitressed there, and she certainly looked like she could take on someone in a bar fight and hold her own.

So what kind of home life did she provide for her boys?

Then there was Ashley—who sat silently at her desk, making minimal effort and exuding the air of a child who wanted to be any place other than school. Yet her perpetual sulky pout and frequent

bored sighs didn't seem like the attitude of someone who would draw violent scenes and hide them
around the classroom.

If Ashley had an issue, Carrie thought with an
inward smile, she would probably march up to a
teacher's desk and make her complaints perfectly
clear.

None of the other kids stood out.

They all participated, to some degree, except for
Noah Colwell, who appeared to be afraid of his
own shadow, but the others seemed as boisterous
and outgoing as any other fifth graders would be;
chattering and joking with each other before and
after class.

From now on, Carrie would watch them like a
hawk and make sure she discovered the identity
of her unknown artist. And if there did seem to be
some concerns, she would definitely follow through,
no matter what Marie said.

Surely Principal Grover couldn't be as callous as
Marie claimed.

FIVE

On Friday, with four drawings in her folder, Carrie guessed there would be a fifth by the time class was over, but she still hadn't seen anyone surreptitiously leave one of them behind. The anonymous artist obviously waited each time until her back was turned.

At five minutes before class ended, she leaned against her desk and smiled. "You're all doing an *amazing* job with your paintings. We'll finish them up on Monday so they can be displayed in the hall, and then we'll start a unit on the influence of American Indian culture on art. Any questions?"

Everyone stirred, clearly eager for the bell to ring.

"I have one for you, then. I've found some wonderful drawings in the room—really well done. But I don't know who did them, and would like to give them back to the right person." She briefly held up one of the drawings, then slipped it back in the manila folder. "Does anyone know who did them?"

Some of the students looked around at each other, while others just gave her a blank stare.

"No one? Well, if the artist wants to talk to me privately, that's fine, too. Have a great afternoon, everyone."

Right on cue, the school bell rang and the students flooded out the door.

With a sigh, she gathered up the folder and strode to the main office, where Dottie, the silver-haired school secretary, greeted her with a warm smile. "How's it going?"

"I'm really happy to be here. The town is charming."

"And busy." Dottie chuckled. "Now that the tourist season is under way, Main is nearly impassable, but come September things will go back to normal."

"Is Mr. Grover available? I have a few questions for him."

Dottie glanced out the window toward the parking lot. "He left just a minute ago, but you might be able to catch him. Or you can leave a message with me."

The message left for him yesterday hadn't done much good, so Carrie shook her head. "I'll see if I can catch him outside. Otherwise, I can just wait until next week. Thanks."

She hurried out the door and down the sidewalk, reaching the parking lot just as the principal stepped off the curb by a gray Ford Focus. Tall, with thinning brown hair, wire rims and a paunchy midsection, he had the weary air of someone who needed to retire. And from what Marie had said about him, that day was long past due.

"Mr. Grover, could I bother you for just a second?"

He paused and frowned. "Is it important? I'm meeting my wife for lunch."

"Really, this will just take a moment. I'm a little worried about someone in my class—"

He gave a bored sigh. "The pictures. I know."

"You do?" Carrie's heart lifted. Maybe this was an ongoing situation and was already being addressed.

"Marie told me about your concerns. Really, this type of drawing is very typical for boys this age. Just like she told you, they're intrigued by weapons and battles, and most of them go through a phase of drawing this stuff. It's like a rite of passage." He snorted. "Given the tremendous violence of the video games they're allowed to play, it's no surprise."

"But it seems—"

"Ms. Randall." There was no mistaking the impatience in his voice. "I realize that you're new at teaching. But this is not an issue. And if it bothers you a great deal, well…"

His voice trailed off, leaving his implication perfectly clear.

"No. It's not that," she said, frustration and disappointment washing through her. Marie had been right after all.

He punched a button on his key ring and opened his car door. "Good, then. See you on Monday."

She stepped back and watched him drive away.

Had she been foolish, making more of something than she should have? Was it worth jeopardizing her contract to pursue it further?

The principal had made that risk clear, yet a still, small voice in her heart called out a warning, urging her to not let this go. *Please, God, let me know what to do.*

Saturday dawned bright and clear, with a chilly breeze typical in the mountains during the first half of June. Pausing as he worked at patching a spare raft, Logan breathed in the incomparable sweet scents of pine and damp earth.

Snowdrifts still persisted in shaded places, though the delicate buttercups, spring crocus and crimson paintbrush were already blooming in abundance in the meadows, and now rafting customers had a good chance at seeing the other signs of spring— like newborn bear cubs, or moose calves.

It couldn't be more different from the heat and dust of a rodeo arena, and for the first time, he found himself almost wishing that he could leave the circuit for good.

As if that were a choice.

His attorney had been worth every cent, but now Logan would be riding broncs a lot longer than he'd intended to…and already, his old injuries made him feel twice his age on cold mornings.

Doc Henderson had said another bad crash in the arena could disable him for good, but the chances of that were slim no matter what Penny thought. It was a risk he'd just have to ignore.

At the sound of approaching footsteps, Logan looked up and saw Carrie making her way across the rocky shoreline to stand at the water's edge.

She was dressed in faded jeans and a moss-green T-shirt knotted at her trim waist, her glossy hair shimmering in the sunlight. She looked like one of the woodland sprites in the painting Penny had kept on her bedroom wall since she was a child.

Just looking at Carrie made him want to run his fingers through that beautiful hair. Made him want to whisk her away to someplace where they could talk and get to know each other a lot better, away from the intermittent hustle and bustle of this place.

But that was a bad idea.

She hadn't fled after he told her about Sheryl's death and the trial—which was incredible in itself—though she'd been carefully formal and distant ever since, offering a polite wave or nod if they happened to cross paths.

He knew she left for school by seven in the morning and didn't return until almost two. Afterward, she worked on lesson plans, according to Penny, or left again in her SUV to head for the endless miles of hiking trails in the area. She had yet to go anywhere in the evening, though…and disappeared into her apartment with the windows closed and shades drawn before nightfall. So what was up with that?

Not that it was any of his business, and he planned to keep it that way.

As if sensing his attention, she turned away from the river and sauntered up to him. "Penny says you have just one raft guide hired for the summer."

Warning bells sounded in his head. "That's right. Tina and Penny both take groups down the river. I do, too, in a pinch."

"But you have three rafts, and she says there'll be times when you're shorthanded."

He hesitated, then nodded.

"I'd like to work for you, if you need a spare guide. My afternoons and weekends are free." She lifted a delicate shoulder. "Future summers, too, once school is out each year."

He hid a smile at her naiveté. She had *no* idea how tough it was to manage a big, bulky raft with a load of people…or about the endless hours of training it took to get to that point. "I appreciate the offer, but it's a lot harder than you think."

She didn't bother trying to hide her own smile in response. "I do have some idea."

"This river has some Class I sections, but even if you've been white-water rafting before, the wilder stretches are dangerous. Right now, with spring runoff, they're up to a strong Class IV, and the river channels are changing all the time. Have you been rafting before?"

"California Salmon River, Class V. Colorado River, Grand Canyon."

He whistled. "Those must have been exciting vacations."

She tipped her head in agreement.

"But being a passenger and being a guide are two different things. The responsibility…"

Penny rounded the corner with an armload of life jackets and plopped them on the ground next to the raft. "I see you two are getting things settled, then. Glad to have you on board, Carrie. We need the help."

Startled, Logan looked between Carrie and his sister. "Wait a minute—"

Penny beamed. "I actually had to sort of talk her into it, but we are *so* lucky. I had no idea that she'd been a raft guide before. And experienced guides usually just want to hire on with the bigger companies."

Eyeing Carrie's petite build, Logan felt his mouth drop open. If she could handle a kayak on a glass-calm lake, he'd be surprised. "Experienced? *Her?*"

"It isn't all about brawn," Penny retorted, her eyes sparkling. "I don't suppose you asked her, but she put herself through college working as a raft guide on the Snake."

He blinked. "The Snake."

"Jackson Hole area."

"I do know where it is." He felt a new sense of respect for the young teacher standing in front of him, though for the life of him he still couldn't imagine her having the required strength. The Snake was beautiful, but its changing channels could be fast and treacherous in the spring, and had even claimed a number of lives in recent years.

Penny toed one of the life jackets. "I know you'll want to check out her skills, so if you two want to take a trial run, go right ahead. Tina and I can handle everything here for a while. And hey, it might even be a good chance to get to know each other. Honestly, I've never in my life seen two people trying so hard to ignore each other. I think you'd find each other to be good company."

Uncomfortable, Carrie looked away.

She'd expected that she'd need to demonstrate her river skills, but she'd been thinking that Penny or Tina would go with her because they were the guides who were on the river the most. The *last* thing she wanted was to face those hours alone with Logan.

Sure, the water was fast and high. Reading the currents, channels and hazards of an unfamiliar river would require fast decisions and decisive maneuvers, leaving little time for awkward conversation.

But since she'd come to terms with her concerns about his past, her traitorous heart had gone back to its old routine—with that little extra skip every time she saw him, along with an unwanted sense of extra awareness that had no place in their strictly business relationship.

And she definitely wanted nothing more than that.

She'd already succumbed to foolish attraction once before and had discovered that she was apparently a poor judge of character. And where had it gotten her? A precipitous marriage to Billy, and after it was over, she'd ended up watching the shadows and fearing the night, regretting her poor judgment. It would be a long, long time before she had any interest in taking that risk again. Distance *was* the best policy.

Though from the pained expression in his eyes, Logan had little desire for greater proximity, either. Exactly how she felt…so why did his cool reserve rankle?

He cleared his throat. "Sounds like a good plan, Penny—except I have an appointment at the bank at eleven, and they close at noon so I can't be late. You'll have to go with her instead."

"I have two two-hour float trips scheduled today." Penny folded her arms across her chest and frowned. "You could reschedule that appointment."

"Nope. It's with Rob Peters, the loan officer. He's leaving on vacation later this afternoon. Tina—"

"Has to watch the office while I'm on the river, so she can collect the money and release forms from the second set of customers today. Then she has to bus them down to Hawk Landing so they can board, and bus the first group back up here."

Logan thought for a moment. "We'll also need to check with the insurance company about adding another guide."

"Don't worry about it," Carrie murmured, backing away. "I…um…have lesson plans to work on and errands to run. Penny can just let me know when she has the time…or we can forget about it altogether. It doesn't really matter to me."

Penny frowned. "But you said you'd be interested in some hours, right?"

"Yes, but—"

"If you could handle the office this afternoon, that would be great. As a guide you'd be getting tips, but at least this would be an extra paycheck. And if things are slow, you can work on your lesson plans in the office."

"That would be fine."

"Good. Then we can sort out the other issues later." Penny gave her brother a long, pointed look. "After Logan and I sit down for a talk, I'm sure we can get this settled."

SIX

Carrie hesitated on the steps of the Granite Falls Community Church and glanced at the sign listing service times, needing an extra moment or two to settle the butterflies in her stomach.

She'd always loved old churches, and had admired this white clapboard church with its towering steeple and tall stained-glass windows along both sides of the sanctuary when she'd first come to town for her interview.

But this was her first Sunday service here. She hardly knew anyone in town. Light rain was falling, so no one was standing around to visit on the sidewalk, and already she felt like an awkward outsider. *But this is about You and me, God. Right? It isn't a social occasion.*

Taking a fortifying breath, she pulled open the massive oak door and stepped into the small crowd of people chatting quietly just inside. Ahead, through an open set of double doors leading into the nave, a center aisle led to the altar, with oak pews on either side.

"Ms. Randall!" Rachel, one of her students, side-stepped through the gathering with a middle-aged brunette in tow. "This is my mom, Ivy Graham."

"What a nice surprise," Carrie murmured, offering her hand. "Rachel is a fine student. I'm so glad to have her in my class."

"She talks a lot about you." Ivy smiled warmly. "There are several of your students who attend here, actually." She craned her neck to search, then waved a hand toward a tall, barrel-chested man at the far end of the entryway. "There's Garrett's dad. Have you met him?"

"Not yet. Is Noah here?"

"Now, that's hard to say. He's such a quiet little guy—not that I blame him." She craned her neck. "Ah—see over there, by the water fountain? There he is. And the redhead next to him is his aunt Linda Bates. She's been living with her brother and Noah since Sheryl died."

As if they'd heard her words, Noah and his aunt both looked in her direction. Linda's eyes widened when Noah tugged on her sleeve and whispered something, then the two of them hurried away from the entry toward a side exit.

Oblivious to their departure, Ivy continued to survey the other churchgoers. "There's Margaret, from down at the bank...and Oscar Nelson—he owns the drugstore. Oh, and there's one of the deputies in town. Have you met Rick Peterson?"

Surprised, Carrie looked across the room and caught sight of the tall, slender deputy. "Briefly."

Dressed in a white polo shirt and khaki slacks instead of his crisply starched uniform, he still wore a military aura of command. "He's the older brother of one of my high school classmates." She winked. "Come with me. It's always nicer to visit with someone if he isn't giving you a traffic ticket, don't you think?"

Carrie followed Ivy across the entryway. "We did meet, but it wasn't over a traffic violation."

"Oh, that's right." Ivy's hand flew to her mouth, a pink tinge climbing up her face. "There was some sort of…a *domestic* call, wasn't it? I heard it on the scanner."

"You and everyone else in the county, apparently." Carrie offered a wry smile. "But it wasn't a domestic issue. I saw a prowler and called 911."

Clearly flustered, Ivy blushed a deeper pink. "I'm so sorry. I didn't mean to pry, or anything…I spend more time with my feet in my mouth than anyone I know."

The soft sweet strains of "Beautiful Savior" began, and the stragglers in the entryway all headed toward the pews. The deputy started to follow, until he glanced over at Ivy and turned back. "Mornin', Ivy," he said, his voice soft and warm.

Until now, Carrie had only seen him in his terse

cop mode, but if the man wasn't carrying a torch for Rachel's sweet mom, Carrie would be surprised.

"Rick, I believe you two have met briefly once before, but under less pleasant circumstances. This is the new teacher in town, Carrie Randall," Ivy whispered. "Carrie, this is Deputy Rick Peterson." She looked between them and smiled, then backed away. "If you'll excuse me, I need to join my mother and the kids."

When Ivy stepped away, the deputy pinned Carrie with a hard, searching look. "Are you still staying out at the Bradley place?"

"I am."

"Any more troubles out there?"

"There were, actually. Someone damaged one of the river rafts."

"Damaged?"

"It looked like it was slashed, actually, with a knife." She met his gaze squarely. "But Logan said it wouldn't do any good to call in a report."

"I hear his rafting company isn't doing so well financially." Rick's cold eyes narrowed. "Things aren't always what they seem, Ms. Randall."

"If you're implying that he did it himself for the insurance claim, you're wrong." She caught the rising emotion in her voice and took a slow breath. "Anyway, he'd want a police report on the vandalism, right?"

Rick snorted in derision. "Maybe he knew we'd see things a little *too* clearly. You do know about the charges against him last year. Right? And the trial?"

"Yes, and the fact that he was acquitted. Seems to me that justice was served."

"Or maybe not. Just remember I warned you," he said in a low voice. "Associating with the bad elements in town can mean you get tarred with the same brush." The pager on his belt hummed. He reached for it, read the screen and turned for the arched front doors of the church. "If I were you, I'd watch my step."

On her way home from church an hour later, Carrie smiled to herself, thankful she'd gone. After the service, Ivy again apologized over her gaffe, then proceeded to introduce Carrie to everyone in sight. She'd already seen many of the members around town or at school, so being able to connect names and faces would help her fit into the fabric of the community.

But the deputy's insinuations had played through her thoughts during the service, and even now she couldn't forget what he'd said. Clichéd or not, his words had held more than a veiled warning about her association with the Bradleys.

Logan hadn't been kidding when he'd said that reporting the damage to the raft wouldn't do him much good because he figured the local sheriff's department probably wouldn't be much help.

And now she had to wonder. If she ever had

trouble with prowlers or stalkers or a certain ex-husband while living at the Bradley place, would they bother to come quickly…or even come at all?

Logan tightened the final strap on the life jacket, then grinned at the elderly man who had been grumbling for the past ten minutes about his wife's decision to go rafting. "It's an easy run, from here down to the fork. You'll think you're in an easy chair back home."

"Right. But if that little girl over there—"

"Tina. She's been river guiding since she was seventeen."

"Well, if she misses that fork, what then?"

"The Wolf is calm to that point. There, she'll take the right fork into Selby Creek and you'll enjoy another five miles of quiet water before you land."

"Hmpf. And if she goes to the left, we die."

"No. The main channel does change to some serious white water. *That* would be more like a cycle through your washing machine. But it won't happen. Promise."

"You'd better be right. She looks about as strong as my twelve-year-old niece."

Tina finished loading the last of four women, then beckoned. "Ready, sir."

Grumbling, the man squared his shoulders as he trudged over to the raft, clearly not wanting to be shown up by his wife and the other silver-haired women who were already on board and chatting gaily about their river adventure.

At the sound of tires crunching on gravel, Logan turned and found Carrie pulling to a stop by the office. She stepped out of her car, pretty as a daffodil in a slim yellow skirt, top and matching jacket, the sunshine picking out golden highlights in her sleek cap of mahogany hair.

He felt his heart stop for just a moment before it remembered to pick up its regular beat.

"Howdy," he called out, knowing it was probably better to get this over now…despite Penny's feelings to the contrary.

Carrie smiled and walked over, slipping out of her jacket and draping it over one shoulder as she crossed the parking area. "Beautiful day for a float," she said, eyeing the elderly group of passengers in Tina's raft. "Are you going out, as well?"

"Later. About the raft guiding…" He cleared his throat. "I checked with our insurance agent. Do you have the certificates for Swift Water Rescue and Wilderness First Responder?"

"That must be something new. I haven't guided since I was in college."

"So you probably just had First Aid and CPR."

She nodded. "And the usual river training, plus four summers of experience."

"Unfortunately, our insurance rates are sky-high as it is, and we're required to supply proof of certification for every guide or they'll double the cost of our policy."

Her face fell. "How soon can I be certified?"

"The First Responder class takes eight days, and the Level I and II Water Rescue classes add up to over four. Not that much—but they're only taught a couple times a year in this area."

"Is it hard to get in?"

"I did some calling. The tuition is pricey for all three, but the June classes start on Monday. During the first four days you'd be doing both classes every day, to get the Water Rescue classes done while you're taking the First Responder series. You could be done by the end of next week, if you were really serious about this. But this is awfully short notice."

"It starts *tomorrow?*"

"Right. And they do have several slots available, so you could still get in."

She cast a wistful look toward the river. "The summers I spent guiding were some of the best in my life. Being out on the river every day, facing the challenges…and I covered a lot of my college tuition with the tips I made, too."

"I can't guarantee a set number of scheduled trips, though."

"Still, it would be a good job for a teacher, since I have my summers off." She considered for a moment. "Would the class times conflict with my morning teaching schedule?"

"They start at one o'clock and end at dusk, so it would work, though it would be a mighty long day." He shrugged, sure that she'd decide against it. Hoping that would be her response.

She bit her lower lip, considering. "I'll do it. It was really sweet of you to check this all out for me."

Sweet? He'd expected her to shy away from such a heavy commitment. He'd *hoped* that she would, because he'd felt an attraction to her since the first day she arrived, and he'd resolved to keep careful distance to avoid any complications. But now, she was looking up at him with a soft smile, and he felt like a complete heel for not encouraging her to do something he knew would make her happy.

"I…well… If you want to go out on the river, you can always come along with the groups if there's an empty place." He cleared his throat. "Though I don't expect you'll have much time during the next couple of weeks. Sometimes Penny or I go out alone in a small raft or take the kayaks, and you'd be welcome to come along then, if you want. Or you can go alone. No charge. I guess you'll need to start learning this river."

Her smile brightened and lit up her hazel eyes. "That would be wonderful. I suppose you can guess that my summer teaching salary doesn't stretch very far."

"About that…Penny and I talked it over. I'm not sure how many raft trips we can promise you this summer because business has been slow. Her offer still stands if you'd like some hours manning the office. She pointed out that having someone here at the office would make everything a lot easier."

"And what about you?"

Her gleaming hair shifted as she tipped her head, studying him. How had he missed the sprinkle of freckles over her nose? Or the way the corners of her mouth tilted up, ever so slightly, even when she wasn't smiling?

He blinked, trying to remember what she'd just said. "What?"

"Do you mind having me around? I get the feeling that you aren't so sure you want me here after all. So if it's just Penny's idea…"

The problem was that he *did* want her around. A lot more. He cleared his throat. "No…I think she's right."

"Then it's a deal."

Carrie proffered her hand and he reached out to shake it. And once again, he felt that little zinging sensation of awareness at her touch. A sensation that warmed his hand and sent sparks speeding toward his calloused heart.

"This will probably work out well," he added. "As it was, we could only have two guides on the river at any given time, since one of us had to stay here at the home base. If you start working for us whenever you have some free time, then maybe I can get back on the road for the rest of the summer and we'll still have two people guiding."

"The *road?*" Her startled eyes flew up to meet his. "Are you a sales rep or something?"

"Rodeo."

Usually, people were curious when he mentioned that part of his life. A lot of the tourists and pretty little buckle bunnies at the rodeos were even star-struck by the cowboys who consistently took home the big paychecks. But Carrie's eyes now widened in obvious horror. Had she misunderstood?

"Saddle broncs," he added, when she didn't respond. "I thought you knew. The pictures up in the office…the bronc saddle on display in the corner?"

"I've only been in there a couple of times. I thought it was all just there for Western atmosphere."

She looked so disappointed that he had to bite back a laugh. "Nope. I grew up on a ranch and com-peted in high school rodeo, so I just kept at it."

"B-but you're operating a *rafting* business."

"This here is my retirement plan. I'm thirty-three—getting old, by rodeo standards. Since the family ranch is long gone, I started saving toward the future a long time ago. Good thing, because I've been laid up for the first two months of this season."

"Rodeo," she repeated glumly.

"As soon as I'm cleared by the doc, I need to catch the rest of the season. It's too late for making the year-end standings, but the money's still good. After this year and next, I'll be able to quit."

She stared at him, silent and still, her face chalk-white. And then she walked away.

SEVEN

Carrie stepped out of her SUV on Monday morning, carefully surveyed the teachers' parking lot, then tapped the lock button on her key ring remote and hurried toward the back entrance of the school.

Everything was at it should be. Students being dropped off by parents at the front door. Some walking from various parts of the small town. Traffic was light in town, since the tourist crowds usually didn't pick up until midmorning. Which should have made it easier to spot anything unusual. Anyone who might have been following her…or waiting somewhere, to watch her pass by.

But something wasn't right.

She'd felt it at the back of her neck. That uneasy prickling sensation of warning. She'd had an uneasy premonition before she ever left her riverside apartment. And she'd had it earlier, when someone called her cell phone twice in the middle of the night but hung up when she answered.

She'd immediately gone to her laptop to trace the

caller's name via a reverse lookup website, but the number had been untraceable.

She'd sighed with relief when Logan, Penny and Tina all drove in and parked over by the boathouse this morning, knowing that she wasn't alone. Yet even now, with students and teachers all funneling into the school, she again had a disquieting sense that she was being watched.

In the relative privacy of her classroom, with the door firmly shut, she called Trace, impatiently counting the rings. The kids were piling up outside the door and she'd have to let them in before Marie or the principal stopped in to see what was going on. Why wasn't he answering?

She shivered, remembering one of Billy's emails from a few months ago. *You're going to be so sorry. Your family, too.*

Trace had laughed off her immediate concern for his safety, but he certainly hadn't wasted a minute where she was concerned. He'd immediately reported the message to both the sheriff's department and Sam Olson, Carrie's lawyer, and demanded that they follow up.

She'd always followed Sam's advice and never responded to any of her ex-husband's calls or messages. Sam had, though, to keep track of his whereabouts, but Billy had dropped out of sight for many months.

But then there'd been the email he sent to her just a few weeks ago, promising that he'd be paying her a visit soon. Would he? He'd taunted her before and hadn't followed through. Surely he knew that he'd gain nothing but trouble if he harassed her now.

But could she stake her life on it?

And soon, she might be even more vulnerable, if Logan went traipsing off to follow the rodeo circuit. *Rodeo.*

It had been a startling revelation, to say the least, and had effectively doused any attraction she felt toward him.

The last thing she needed in her life was a foot-loose, irresponsible cowboy chasing the sunsets across the country. Perhaps absence made the heart grow fonder, but distance also set the stage for lies and deceit that were hard to detect.

Logan probably wasn't like Billy at all. There were plenty of honest, good-hearted cowboys out there—many who even belonged to Cowboys for Christ, and who would share her faith.

But even worse than Billy's lies and hot temper were the sleepless nights and the worry. The years of fearing the ring of the phone, afraid Billy had been injured…or killed, like his buddy Mike two years ago. She could never live that life of fear again. Ever.

She heard a faint click, then Trace's recorded voice came on. She left a brief message. Switched the phone to vibrate. Then dropped it into the pocket of her ivory slacks, straightened her crimson summer top and dredged up a smile as she walked to the door.

With luck, Trace would text her back with the news she wanted to hear. And soon. But if not…

Her hand on the doorknob, she bowed her head for a moment in silent prayer. And then she opened the door for the waiting children and started her day.

She'd worried and fidgeted all day Monday, waiting for Trace to call. By the time her cell phone finally vibrated at six o'clock, in the middle of her Wilderness First Responder class, her nerves were jangled and the phone slipped out of her hand twice when she tried to pull it out of her pocket. When she saw his fiancée's number, not his, on the caller ID, her heart nearly stopped. "Is everything all right, Kris? Where is Trace—is he okay?" she whispered, turning away from the rest of the group.

"Never better," he drawled.

"Trace." Weak with relief, Carrie felt her heart drop. "I've been worried about you all day."

"As well you should. We spent the whole day looking at tuxes and wedding flowers up in Billings. I think I'd rather be run over by a bull than ever do that again."

"You didn't get my message. Where's your phone?"

"I left it on Kris's kitchen counter, but we're almost back there now. What's up?"

She hesitated. She'd had no trouble all day. There'd been no sign of anyone stalking her when she left school at noon. Should she even say anything? Was her foolish imagination just playing tricks on her?

But her message was still on Trace's phone, waiting to be heard, and there was no way to take it back.

"I…well, I had a couple of hang-up calls last night. I just get this uneasy feeling now and then that someone is watching me. And…well, I've had a prowler at night. Twice."

He was silent for a moment. "You called the sheriff, right?"

"I did…but there hasn't been much to go on. The guy uses one of those cheap, preloaded phones that you can buy at Walmart, so his calls are untraceable. I haven't seen his face."

"Billy couldn't possibly know where you are, sis. Only Kris and I do, and we haven't told a soul."

"I know you wouldn't." She fiddled with the frayed hem of her jeans. "But you haven't seen him around Battle Creek, have you? Or heard anything?"

"Kris looked up the Southwest rodeo standings last night. He's listed as being out of the money at a couple of rodeos in New Mexico during May."

"But nothing since then?"

"If he wasn't even making gas and entry money, maybe he took a job on a ranch somewhere just to build up some cash. He's done that before."

"True." But he definitely wouldn't be happy about it. "So nothing on the lists since May?"

"Maybe she should check the surrounding states. He could've moved on."

"I could do that myself, too. But thanks, Trace. It's good to hear your voice."

"Maybe you should just come back to the ranch," he added quietly. "I hope you consider this your home, too."

But it wasn't the family ranch they'd grown up on. Trace had bought the Rocking R himself and had built it up to the success it was today, and soon it would be his new bride's home, as well. A sister hanging around forever would be like an old spinster aunt at a party—just in the way.

Carrie fiddled with the delicate silver bracelet that he'd given her when she turned eighteen. "I have a full-time job here in the fall, and I'm contracted for summer session now. I can't give that up. I've wanted this for too long."

"But I still have that empty cabin for you, and you'd be safer here no matter what. Think about it."

"I will. Thanks, Trace."

She held the phone long after he disconnected the call. After class was over at nine, she'd go home and start some research on the internet. With luck, she'd find Billy listed among the rodeo money earners on some other rodeo circuit: happy, busy and far, far away. But that posed still another worry.

If Billy wasn't lurking in Granite Falls, then who could be stalking her—and why?

White-knuckling the steering wheel of her SUV, Carrie eyed the gas gauge on the instrument panel and said another silent prayer as she drove the last two miles home after her White-water Rescue class.

Her tank had been over three-quarters full when she'd driven out to the site of the class, four miles on the other side of Granite Falls. She'd been *sure* of it. Yet her low-fuel light had come on when she started the vehicle afterward, and with the two gas stations in town already closed for the evening, she'd been biting her fingernails the rest of the way home.

The gauge had always been accurate.

There was no way she could've used that much gas.

And there couldn't have been a leak—there'd been no pungent odor of gasoline surrounding the vehicle when she'd climbed back in. So who would come out in the middle of nowhere to siphon fuel? It wouldn't have been difficult to pull it off, if someone was desperate or otherwise motivated, though.

The instructors and students always parked at the side of the rutted, narrow access road leading to the river, and she'd been the last one to pull in. There'd been the usual half-hour discussion before everyone traipsed down the path to the river for several hours of hands-on demonstration and practice on a stretch of white water. All the while, the vehicles were out of sight, and the noisy river would've masked the sound of anyone driving up the lane.

At the sign for Wolf River Rafting she breathed a sigh of relief, flipped on her turn signal and turned in. Had she been targeted…or simply a random victim?

Either way, the sense of being violated made her shiver. What if she'd run out of gas somewhere between here and town? With just intermittent cell phone service thanks to the mountains, it might have been a very long and lonely walk.

A pair of headlights flashed in her rearview mirror, swung around and blinded her for a split second, then a motor gunned and the vehicle took off down the highway with a squeal of tires. Her heart lodged in her throat at the obvious implication.

A coincidence? Not likely. She'd been followed.

By someone who'd expected to find her stranded on the highway and vulnerable—though fortunately he'd misjudged the amount of fuel it would take for that to happen.

Her fear faded and her anger grew. She was tired of this. Tired of being followed, of being threatened, of not knowing for sure who was behind it all.

It wasn't right, and it wasn't fair that some unknown stranger was threatening her future and possibly even her life, when all she wanted was a chance to start over and finally be happy.

And if it turned out to be Billy, she wouldn't give

in to her old feelings and back away from pressing charges. Not this time. Not ever again. Whatever her intentions for the future were, however brave she felt at this moment with the threat now gone, it was still terrifying to be confronted with danger in the dark and all alone.

Thank You, God, for watching out for me, she murmured as she stepped on the accelerator and tried to calm her shaking nerves.

In minutes, she pulled in close to the rafting office, grateful for the security light that lit her stairway and the lamp glowing in the boathouse window.

She hesitated. Scanning the vicinity for any movement, she felt her tension ease when the boathouse door swung open and Logan appeared.

"Glad to see you," she called out as she stepped from her SUV and hit Lock on her key ring.

He strode over to her, frowning as he pulled to a stop and searched her face. "You look so pale. Everything all right?"

"I think I may have been followed here…possibly by someone who also drained most of the fuel from my gas tank." She gave him a quick summary. "If this was Billy, he ought to know better. And if it's someone else—the big question is *why?*"

"I think you should call the sheriff."

"I thought about it—but what proof do I have of anything? They probably already think I've cried wolf one too many times as it is."

His expression troubled, Logan slowly shook his head. "Maybe I should start taking you to those classes."

A warm feeling unfurled in her heart at the deep concern in his eyes. "And to school, back and forth on all of these trips? It's sweet of you to offer, but it's also impractical. I'll—I'll just be more careful."

"And how will you do that? It's impossible to protect yourself every minute." He rested his large, strong hands on her shoulders. "Maybe you need a bodyguard."

"Very funny." She gave a short laugh. "Me. A part-time teacher, without fame or fortune. Or any real enemies, for that matter."

"I'm serious."

His intent gaze locked on to hers and she could no more look away than she could have stopped the moon's orbit. His eyes were so beautiful, filled with such compassion and concern, that she felt safer than she had in a long, long time. "Thanks. But just having you here makes me feel better."

His hands slid slowly down her arms and captured her hands. "I do know it's impractical to have someone watching over you day and night. But at least give Penny or me a call whenever you go somewhere so we'll know where you've gone and when you plan to be back."

"I can't expect you to—"

"Yes, you can." With a low growl tinged with frustration, he pulled her gently into a warm, comforting hug.

Well—maybe that was the intent.

Instead, warm tingles of awareness rushed through her at the wonderful sensation of being held in his strong arms, and when she breathed in his unique, masculine scent of pine, fresh air and a faint hint of woodsy aftershave she felt as though she'd come home. She stilled, wanting the moment to last. Knowing she should step away. Wondering what it would be like if he dropped his mouth to hers for a kiss.

When he abruptly released her and stepped back, his breathing ragged and his expression dazed, she knew he'd been affected, as well.

"I...I'd better go," she faltered, thankful that the darkness hid the warm blush climbing up her cheeks. "I...have assignments to grade and...um... it's late."

"Keep your cell phone by your bedside," he warned. "Call me if *anything* seems suspicious."

He waited until she went inside, then slowly turned away after she waved to him from a window.

She'd brushed aside his concern, not wanting him to feel obligated. Not wanting to be a burden. Knowing, after a lifetime of experience, that the one person she needed to rely on was herself. But his concern had echoed her own, and now, in her empty apartment—save for one sleeping cat—she glanced around and felt the walls closing in on her.

God—I know You're here with me. Help me feel Your strength and Your presence, and to remember that I'm really never alone.

Long after she'd settled into her apartment for the night and finished grading the papers, Carrie roamed her rooms, unable to settle down. Unable to let go of a premonition that had been tying her stomach into knots.

A few hang-up phone calls and unfounded worries about her ex-husband were hardly proof of trouble, she reminded herself as she settled back down at her desk and turned on her laptop. Billy was probably somewhere in New Mexico, and her foolish imagination was simply working overtime.

Since she couldn't sleep, she might as well email Trace and Kris, and ask about how their wedding plans were coming along. Catch up with some old school friends on her social-networking websites... or even work on her lesson plans for next week. After an hour or two, she ought to be able to fall asleep without any problem at all.

She opened her email program, slid the cursor over to New Messages. Clicked. And felt her heart lodge in her throat.

A long list of incoming messages filled the page.

And every last one of them was from Billy.

EIGHT

Internet service at Wolf River was painstakingly slow. Halfway through trying to get something done online, she often found herself disconnected and needing to start all over again. The only people she'd likely hear from outside of Granite Falls were Trace and Kris at any rate, and they'd call her cell phone before bothering to type out a message.

But now, given the emails she'd received from Billy last night, the antiquated internet connection was more frustrating than ever, and it was past time to leave for school. Carrie drummed her fingernails on her kitchen table as she glanced through the first few messages, forwarding each one to Sam before she deleted them.

We need to talk...

Things have been tough. About that bank loan I had...

You'll be seeing me soon. You owe me...

You're in real trouble...

The internet disconnected. Again. Exasperated, she hit the off button on her laptop and slammed the cover shut. The emails were just more of the same, and her lawyer could deal with him. She'd send the rest later.

There'd been few assets to divide during the divorce. No real estate. No investments to speak of. Billy had actually tried to go after her for support, since she was the only one of them who had a regular paycheck. He'd hammered home the fact that she had a brother who owned a "fancy ranch," as if it meant she had access to money that Billy deserved.

Her fear faded, and renewed anger took its place. No harassment, subtle or otherwise, was going to help him win anything from her. He was welcome to try.

Though still, a small voice of warning niggled at her, chipping away at her flash of bravado and reminding her of what it had been like to live with his volatile temper...

And of the fact that she was out here very much alone.

When her rafting certification classes were cancelled on Tuesday and Wednesday, Carrie reported to the raft company office. Penny, Tina and Logan were booked solid into the evening, so Carrie's own afternoon flew while she handled the customers, collected liability release forms and outfitted each set of passengers with the appropriate gear.

While waiting for the final float trip to return, she set up her laptop in the office and finished forwarding Billy's emails to Sam without bothering to read them. She hadn't heard back from Sam about the first set, but still felt a flash of relief when the task was done. "So there, Billy Danvers," she muttered under her breath. "Take *that*."

"You don't sound happy." A low laugh rumbled from the door of the office, and Logan walked in. "You always talk to your computer in that voice?"

"It isn't the computer. It…was just some business I had to take care of."

Lifting an eyebrow, he sauntered up to her desk and settled into a chair. "The only time I've heard that edge in your voice has been over that ex-husband of yours. Is he causing you any trouble?"

"Long distance. Which is enough. So how did your raft trip go?" She glanced at the open schedule book on the desk. "Since you had the white-water group this time, it had to be more fun."

"Yep. Good set of folks, too. They loved it, and not one of 'em did anything crazy. Half said they were coming back again next week." Bracing his elbows on the arms of the chair, he studied her. "So what's this about Billy? Are you expecting trouble?"

"He'd like me to think that."

"Did he call?"

"Emailed. Quite a few times, and he ought to know better."

"It has to be tough, dealing with this."

"It isn't exactly how I expected my marriage to end, believe me." She sighed. "I really meant the 'till death do us part' passage of my marriage vows. I made them in church, before God and my family. It was supposed to be a lifetime bond. And now here I am, divorced and worrying about my ex-husband showing up."

Logan nodded. "Sometimes life just throws us a curve." He looked as if he wanted to say more, but held back.

"It's strange. My marriage was a mistake, I know that now. I fell for charm and a devilish smile, not substance. But I'm not angry anymore…it's more like deep sorrow. Guilt, too. Could I have done something better? Tried harder? If I'd given it more time, could I have changed him? Maybe I failed him as well as myself, you know?"

"If he didn't change just being married to you and wanting to make you happy, then you couldn't have *made* it happen."

She considered his words. "I did learn that if I ever follow my heart, it will only happen with someone who is a good, solid man who shares my faith."

"No more wild and crazy cowboys, then."

"Exactly. It won't be the excitement of some bad boy who lives on the edge of danger, and risks his life every day. And it won't matter if he's not tall, dark and handsome, either. It will be all about what he's like *inside*."

"Sounds like a good plan." Logan's smile didn't quite reach his eyes. "So what did Billy say in those emails?"

"Nothing new." She shrugged. "I didn't even read the last few. I just forwarded everything to my lawyer and deleted the messages. If he has anything to say he can say it to Sam."

"But he could still come looking for you, and I'm not always around." Logan studied her for a long moment. "You should move to town, where you'd have lots of people close by 24/7."

"Billy is probably three states away. And anyway, letting him affect my decisions is no longer something I'm willing to do. Period. I really do like my apartment here."

Logan's eyebrows drew together. "But I don't think it's worth the risk to stay here. Not when I can't guarantee your safety."

"You sound like my brother."

He smiled at that. "Well…maybe that's a good thing."

"So both of you think I'm supposed to run like a scared bunny the rest of my life?" She dredged up a rueful grin at the sharp edge in her voice. "Sorry. I know you're just trying to help."

"I'll start leaving my dog here at night, then."

She'd thought about asking him to do just that,

until she'd seen Murphy's absolute devotion to Logan. The dog seemed to doze the days away, but had a special connection where Logan was concerned. The poor animal whined and paced the shore whenever Logan left on float trips, and only settled down to doze in the shade when he saw his master return.

"I think Murphy would cry all night if you did that."

"Not if he was in your apartment."

"Well…"

"What, you don't like my dog?"

"He's a *great* dog. But—"

"Let's try it tonight. Penny and I could even start taking turns at staying out here, too—there's a sofa in the office downstairs. Or one of us could even bring a sleeping bag and stay out in the boathouse for a while."

"No, though I do appreciate the offer."

"Look at it this way—we won't get any sleep wondering about what's going on out here." A smile kicked up one corner of his mouth. "So we might as well."

She threw up her hands in mock surrender. "Okay—the dog. You and your sister don't need to babysit me out here."

"But you have our phone numbers, right?"

"Still do." She patted the cell phone holder on her belt. "My brother has them also—I hope that's okay. I figured it might be a good backup in case he really needs to contact me. My cell provider doesn't have the best coverage up here."

"That's fine. And you have us on speed dial, right?"

She laughed at that. "I will. Promise."

He rested a warm, strong hand on her shoulder, locking his gaze on hers. The intense expression of concern in his eyes nearly stole her breath away. "I… We're just worried about you, Carrie. So don't take any chances."

Long after their talk, Logan was still out at the boathouse, lights blazing through the windows and open doorway. Now and then Carrie could hear the pounding of a hammer and the whine of a table saw. By midnight, the sounds ceased and the lights in the boathouse were out, but Logan's truck was still parked by the door so he must have settled in for the night out there.

She'd returned to the windows a dozen times or more during the evening, warmed by Logan's presence. Knowing that he was lingering out of concern for her, even though he'd had a long, hard day…and even when he'd left his dog in her care, which should have been enough.

Billy, for all his cowboy charm and courtly manners when they'd been dating, hadn't been half as concerned when she'd had to drive to work on dangerous winter roads, or had been alone during the long months he was gone following one rodeo circuit or another.

Murphy started whining at two in the morning.

She must have fallen asleep, because now she jerked up, pillows falling from the sofa, feeling bleary and disoriented. Murphy was at one of the windows, his nose pushed through the side of the blinds and his paws on the windowsill, the hair raised along his backbone and his tail rigid.

She stumbled over to him, a hand at her throat. "What's up, buddy?"

Murphy growled.

Logan's truck was still out there. Nothing stirred.

A beam of light bobbed inside the boathouse, then Logan appeared at the door with a flashlight. The light arced across the parking lot, then the pine-walled perimeter of the clearing as he strode into the darkness. She held her breath, realizing the danger he could be in if someone was out there lying in wait.

She'd been determined—no, stubborn and selfish—about staying out here, and thinking only of herself. What if he was hurt...or worse?

And there wasn't just the possibility of a human intruder. There were grizzlies out there—bears that wouldn't hesitate to attack if a human inadvertently came up on them in the dark. Moose were even more unpredictable and just as dangerous, and she'd heard there were plenty of both in the area.

"Come on, Murphy. Go find Logan." She snapped her fingers and opened the door, and the dog shot down the stairs, his tail wagging. At least with Murphy at his side, Logan would have some warning. And until she saw both of them return to the boathouse, she wasn't going to move away from the window.

Logan and his dog had been out patrolling the property until nearly one o'clock last night. Carrie had stayed at her window, tense and breathless, murmuring a litany of prayers for his safety, until she'd seen both of them trudge back to the boathouse. At the doorway he'd looked up at her window, given her a thumbs-up signal, then the two of them had disappeared inside.

She had no doubt that the boathouse had offered little in the way of comfort and that he was far more tired than she, but when she got in her car to head for school in the morning, he was already out on the riverbank, talking to two tourists who apparently wanted to go down the river.

When she returned after teaching school, he'd just pulled in from another raft trip. As soon as he saw her, he walked over and gave her shoulders a quick hug.

"Everything okay?"

She felt her heart warm at his concern. "Good. But you're the one who was outside so late. You must be exhausted."

Luckily, the final two float trips of the day both ended at five o'clock, and the last of the passengers were out of the parking lot a half hour later. As soon as the equipment was stowed away, Tina waved goodbye and headed for her pickup, and Logan took off for some supplies in Billings.

"Thanks for helping out, Carrie." Penny looked at her watch. "We're actually done a little early today, and the theater in town changes its shows on Tuesdays. Want to grab some dinner in town and catch a movie afterward?"

"Sounds like fun."

"We could meet at my aunt's place in town at six or so, then go to Northern Lights Steak House—a little pricier but fabulous—or Lindy's, good food, woodsy atmosphere. You choose."

"My heart says Northern Lights. But…"

"Lindy's it is." Penny grinned. "I don't know when I last had a night out like this. I'll send Logan a text message. If he gets back in time, maybe he'll want to join us."

Dinner, a movie. Harmless good times with friends and nothing more. "Um…that sounds fine."

Penny eyed her closely. "Are you sure?"

"Of course. Sort of a coworker night out, right?"

"Exactly." Penny paused at the door of her truck and looked back. "We can leave Murphy with Aunt Betty for the evening, then you can pick him up on your way home so you don't need to come back here alone."

Carrie glanced around, remembering just how quiet this place was when everyone was gone. Even if she'd been longing for an early night, it would be nice not to spend it by herself. "Good idea."

Carrie waved as Penny drove away, then leaned down to give Murphy's shaggy neck a hug. "You need a bath, buddy, if you're visiting Aunt Betty, and then I need a shower. I guess we'd better get moving."

Dinner at the rustic little restaurant overlooking a rushing mountain stream—a crispy Caesar salad, perfectly grilled rib eye and a fluffy baked sweet potato slathered in cinnamon butter—was perfect.

Now they walked out of the small family-run theater with its uneven wood floors and movie memorabilia on the walls from its early days back in the thirties, and slowed to a halt in front as several dozen other patrons drifted away.

"I guess I forgot to mention that they run mostly vintage and second-run family movies here," Penny said. "And the titles on the marquee don't always match what's running inside. Gramps Anderson doesn't like climbing the ladder much anymore, and all his grandkids have moved away. The locals don't think about it."

Carrie grinned. "I've always liked Maureen O'Hara and John Wayne in *McLintock*. The real butter on the popcorn was wonderful, and I never thought I'd get to see that film on a big screen. It's been a wonderful night."

Both of them turned on their cell phones at the same moment, then looked at each other and laughed when both phones instantly emitted goofy rings indicating phone messages.

"Logan," Penny said after listening to her messages. She glanced up and down the sidewalk. "He got a late start out of Billings, but hoped he'd get back in time to meet us at Francie's Ice Cream Parlor after the show. I don't see him yet, but maybe he's already there."

Their shoes thunking on the old-fashioned wooden boardwalk, they fell in step and headed toward the end of the next block, to where a whimsical pink-and-green neon ice cream cone hung out over the sidewalk and a mom and two children sat on the bench out in front. A trio of teenagers leaned against the hood of an old Chevy truck parked nearby, and a few stragglers from the theater were following Penny and Carrie toward Francie's.

"Francie's is the hottest place in town," Penny said. "Wait till you try their hot fudge, triple-scoop peppermint bonbon sundae with mixed nuts and real whipped cream."

"Sounds decadent." Carrie checked her own list of missed calls as they walked. "Just Trace and Kris, probably wondering when I can get back to look for my maid of honor dress. I'll follow up with them tomorrow."

"That's sweet. How big of a wedding party will it be?"

"Intimate…just me and one of Trace's friends. Kris and her sister were orphaned as kids, but Emma disappeared into the foster care system years ago. I don't know what happened to the records, but Kris says it's as if she never existed."

"That's so sad."

"It is. Kris has never given up on her search, but hasn't found so much as a clue. My guess is that Emma probably died years ago."

"Kris doesn't believe it?"

"Nope. She says she would know, deep in her heart, if her sister had died. She says she's been praying for just one hint of where to look next."

"How could someone drop from sight like that? It's pretty tough to disappear."

"I know, and Kris has tried everything. These days, you can look up names on the internet and find birth dates, addresses, phone numbers—even legal records with the click of a button and your credit card number."

"The people who decided all that should be available are idiots. It's scary, knowing what's out there."

Carrie nodded. "My next guess is that if Emma is still alive, she doesn't *want* to be found. What a blow that would be, to find out she'd ended up on the wrong side of the law."

They reached the corner of Main and Pine, a dark cross street leading just several blocks in either direction. On the opposite side, along the shadowed wall of Goode's Drug Store, a broad-shouldered masculine form shifted, then moved forward to meet them.

"Logan? I—" Penny's cheerful greeting faltered to a stop.

At the same moment, Carrie felt a prickle of apprehension crawl on spider's feet up the back of her neck. "Billy," she managed to whisper on a resigned sigh.

The moviegoers behind them swung wide and continued on toward the ice cream parlor. Carrie grabbed Penny's sleeve and tugged her back into the brighter light of the streetlamp at the corner.

Billy stepped into their path, his face backlit by the light, but Carrie had no doubt that his mouth was lifted in his familiar, faint sneer.

"You're hard to find, sugar," he drawled. "Imagine your poor husband trying all this time—"

"*Ex*-husband."

"Imagine me, turning up in Battle Creek, looking forward to seeing you. Only you've disappeared." His voice took on a harder edge. "So I had to start hunting. Why'd you do it, just take off like that? We have *history,* babe. We oughta stay in touch."

"I have no plans for that, Billy. You know better."

His hand snaked out to grab her wrist, but she'd expected it and sidestepped his grasp. "Don't touch me."

"Come on, Carrie," he wheeled. "Let's get out of here."

"No. Penny's brother is waiting for us up ahead."

He gave a hard laugh. "Who, Logan? I don't think he's in town. His truck sure isn't."

"How would you know that—or even know who he is?"

Penny shot a startled glance at Carrie and gave Billy a wide berth. No wonder. But just one more block, and they'd be at the only store open at this hour, with other people close by. Witnesses. *Safe*.

Billy moved even quicker, and once again stood in their way, and this time he grabbed Carrie's shoulder, shoving her away from the crosswalk and toward the darkened side street. "I came all this way, and you're being rude. Your little friend can go on home, but you and I need to talk. Now."

Penny hurried on ahead, her cell phone at her ear as soon as she reached the opposite street corner, and Carrie could see her beckoning to someone, as well.

"How long have you been here, Billy?" Carrie said flatly, twisting out of his grasp.

"Long enough. Pretty sweet setup you have

here—nice job, good friends. Another man already sniffing around. You must think you have it made."

"I don't want to argue with you. You need to leave."

"Do I?" he snapped.

"You don't remember that no-contact order? Or the fact that you have some sorry legal history back in Battle Creek and at least three other towns we lived in? Lay a hand on me again and I'll press charges."

"Good luck, 'cause I sure don't see any witnesses. Even so, a slap on the wrist doesn't mean anything."

He moved closer and she took another step back, belatedly realizing that she'd been focused on his expression and words while he'd been subtly herding her down this quiet street, farther out of sight. The one comfort was that he'd chosen this moment, in town. So maybe he *didn't* know where she lived after all.

"How did you even find me here?"

He snickered. "It isn't that hard, when you know who to ask."

But Trace and Kris would never say a word; she was sure of it. And as a lawyer, Sam certainly understood the principles of privileged information.

Which left the possibility of Sam's high school niece, who worked in his office part-time. She was about as giddy as a teenager could be. She might've listened to Carrie's messages on the answering machine in the office, or overheard Sam talking on the phone. And Billy could just about charm the socks off anyone in a skirt, if he tried—especially a naive teen.

"Kierstan?"

His self-satisfied laugh grated on her nerves. "Like I said, it ain't hard."

"Maybe you could tell me exactly want you want. I know it isn't sharing my company."

"Just five grand. Make it ten, and I'll disappear for good. And I'll even throw in some information that could save your life…maybe. Something you really ought to know about someone here."

Which meant he'd probably picked up on a well-worn rumor about Logan. "No dice. It won't do any good to deliver your little threats. You might as well have asked for a million dollars, because I don't have anything to spare."

"But I know you can get it."

"No, I can't."

"Don't play games with me." His voice turned venomous. "I don't have time, and I'm not gonna wait. I—"

At the periphery of her vision, Carrie saw several people approaching. Rachel Graham's mother, Ivy. An older man and a woman, who was probably his wife. Oscar, the pharmacist. And Penny, who had obviously run ahead to round them all up.

And then through them all, a much taller figure

strode into view, emanating such determination and power—so much like the hero in the movie she'd just seen—that she suddenly felt more protected and safe than she'd ever felt before.

Logan.

"Carrie, is this your ex-husband?"

Embarrassment burned through her. "Unfortunately, yes."

Billy shrank back when Logan halted well within Billy's personal space and towered over him, sweeping him with a disparaging glance.

"Now that you have an audience, maybe you'd like to address your exact concerns before you leave town," he growled. "Or do you just like using intimidation to get what you want?"

Billy was a tall, well-built man, but he was no match for Logan and he clearly knew it. He swallowed hard. Took a furtive look to the left and right. "I was just here visiting with my ex-wife."

Logan didn't take his eyes off his quarry. "Carrie, is that right?"

The others had drawn closer, curiosity and a touch of pity for her in their eyes. The truth was so much harder than trying to save face, though it was probably too late for that anyway. She could only imagine the gossip blossoming about the new teacher in town, the next time the locals gathered for coffee at the Silver Bear Café.

"No. He was demanding money. Again. But I

don't have it, and I don't owe him a dime. When we divorced, everything was split equitably."

Logan took another step toward Billy, crowding him until he again took a step back. "So the emails can stop. And the phone calls. And the unwanted visits. I can't tolerate bullying in children, and in a grown man, it's flat disgusting. A man stands on his own two feet. He doesn't come sniveling around, trying to strong-arm a woman into paying his way."

Billy shifted uneasily, and he glanced behind him.

Logan's voice lowered. "So here's your one chance. Get out of here now, before I truly lose my temper."

A patrol car appeared at the corner of Main and Pine. Slowed, then stopped. The officer inside bent over to peer through his passenger-side window, then his door swung open and he stepped out to look over his car roof. He was the burlier of the two local deputies, the friendly one she'd met on her first day in town. Vance Munson.

"I got a call about some trouble. What's going on here?"

Penny glared at Billy. "That was from me. This guy came into town to cause trouble. Maybe you can send him on his way—or even arrest him. He was *threatening* my friend, here."

Billy edged farther back into the shadows, his face pale and his eyes pinned on the deputy.

Now other people were gathering, and Carrie wished she could simply melt into the street. This was escalating into an even bigger scene, and there was no way to stop it.

And once Billy switched into defensive mode, there was no telling what he'd say—but it wouldn't be true, and it wouldn't be good. She turned to look at Billy. "If I were you—"

But during the moment when she'd looked away, Billy had disappeared.

NINE

After Billy slipped away in the dark, Deputy Munson shooed the crowd away and then questioned Carrie and Penny on the street for a few minutes. After promising to file a report and keep an eye out for Billy in the future, he drove off.

Logan followed Carrie and Penny to Aunt Betty's house, where Carrie picked up Murphy and her SUV. Logan followed her out to the rafting company property.

At the foot of the stairs to her apartment, he studied her intently. "You know Billy better than the rest of us. He has to realize that there were witnesses who saw him in town, even if the deputy didn't get a good look at him. He's hardly here on the sly anymore. Will he leave or stick around?"

"I'm not sure." She glanced out at the faint outline of the towering pines rimming the parking lot. The moon was barely a sliver tonight, and the darkness seemed to close in on her from all sides. "I have no doubt that he knows where I live, though. I wouldn't be surprised if he's been lurking around here, debating his next move. But I don't think he'd be foolish enough to come out here tonight—not after being seen by so many people in town."

"I didn't see any headlights behind me."

"And I didn't see any behind me on the highway except yours, either. He couldn't have driven that road with his lights off. It's too dark, and on the hairpin turns he would've ended up over the edge or a ravine somewhere along the way."

"So now his options are limited. He can hang around town, where people might start to think he's a suspicious stranger and point him out…"

"Or he could lie low and watch for me coming and going from school. I don't think he'll risk coming out here again…not after you confronted him face-to-face and made him back down. He did say something about how giving him money 'could save my life'…but that was just another one of his empty threats."

"I wouldn't count on it. Not after seeing his expression, when he thought he could bully you into giving him exactly what he wanted." Logan looked down at her, the faint moonlight shadowing the planes and angles of his lean, rugged face. He rested his hands on her shoulders. "Munson said he'd alert the other officers about keeping an eye out for him, using the description and photo you gave them. But until Billy is gone for sure, I'll be staying in the boathouse at night."

"But—"

"No arguments." A corner of his mouth quirked up in a grin. "It's actually not too bad over there. I may even do some renovating and move in there for good. My cabin is a good hundred years older."

She looked up at him, grateful for his presence. "You are one very sweet guy."

He laughed at that. "Don't tell Penny that. It'll ruin my image."

He started to turn away, then paused, turned back and pulled Carrie into an embrace. "You'll be fine," he whispered against her hair. "We're going to make sure your problems are taken care of, once and for all. And then you won't need to worry anymore."

A sense of warmth rushed through her, clear down to her toes, and she curved her arms around him in response. "Thank you," she breathed.

He pulled back, his arms still around her, and dropped a sweet, gentle kiss on her lips. Lingered.

And then he walked away.

Two nights later, Carrie still had trouble sleeping. Early Saturday morning she remembered seeing the dial of her alarm clock at two, three-thirty and four, her emotions still in a turmoil after the encounter with Billy and the deputy, followed by the most amazing kiss of her entire life.

But she must have finally dozed, because the first unearthly scream made her launch out of bed, dazed and confused, her heart pounding.

The second sent her racing to the window.

Penny's and Logan's vehicles were by the boathouse, along with several other cars—probably tourists who'd arrived early for the seven-o'clock breakfast float trip.

Carrie caught a glimpse of colorful T-shirts moving through the trees close to where the driveway opened up into the parking lot. Another voice cried out, then Penny appeared, herding a group of four or five clearly distraught women out of the trees toward the raft company office.

The hubbub of voices grew louder as they all drew closer, then stopped when Penny ushered them into the office downstairs and shut the door.

It's not my business to interfere, Carrie reminded herself, reining in her immediate impulse to find out what was going on. And it was probably nothing.

Maybe one of the tourists had simply stumbled and sprained an ankle, or had taken sick. Things were obviously under control, and it was time to shower and dress so she could make it to school in time.

Still, Carrie stood at the window feeling unsettled and anxious, a rising sense of dread curling through her midsection when she heard the sound of an approaching siren.

An EMT vehicle came into view, then stopped. A heavyset woman and a lean man, both dressed in navy coveralls emblazoned with EMT across their shoulder blades, climbed out and hurried to the rear of the vehicle, grabbed their gear and disappeared into the trees.

Logan wasn't anywhere to be seen. Was he back in the woods, directing the EMT to someone who was hurt? Or worse, was he the one who was injured?

Images of the stranger who'd lurked by her SUV invaded her thoughts, followed by a frightening premonition that gripped her heart like an icy hand.

Penny had just told her yesterday about an old recluse named Dante, who lived up in the mountains somewhere. What if Dante or Billy had attacked Logan?

It wasn't hard to imagine Logan pursuing someone, or standing his ground.

She'd already let Murphy outside earlier in the morning to do his business, and he'd been blissfully sleeping on the sofa ever since, but now he stood growling at the window, every muscle rigid. "You've got to stay here, boy…I'll be back."

The dog didn't so much as flick an ear. His attention remained riveted on the EMT truck outside.

Please, Lord, don't let this mean he senses that something terrible has happened. Please, let Logan be all right.

Numb, already afraid of what she was going to find, she pulled on a sweatshirt and a pair of jeans, jammed her feet into loafers, and then she jerked open her front door and started to run.

TEN

Carrie was halfway across the parking lot when she heard the discordant wail of even more sirens approaching.

Logan appeared at the edge of the clearing, his shirt covered with blood and his shoulders slumped in an expression of…defeat? He acknowledged her with only a faint nod when she reached his side.

"What happened?" She resisted the urge to run her hands over his arms and chest, to search for wounds. Someone, or something, had been badly hurt. "Are you all right?"

"A man was shot," he said finally, his voice bleak and raw. "I tried to help, but…it was no use. The EMTs say he was probably gone before they even took over. They're with the body now."

"Oh, Logan."

He looked so devastated that she stepped forward to wrap her arms around him and offer comfort, but he glanced down at his clothes, still glistening with blood, and held up his hands to keep her at bay. "Don't."

"I'm so sorry. Who was it—do you know?"

"I...can't be sure."

But from the haunted expression in his eyes, he probably had a good idea. "Could it be that old guy Penny mentioned—Dante?"

"I don't think so."

Fingers of icy horror crawled up the back of her neck. "You don't *think* so?"

"This guy..." he looked at the ground, clearly measuring his words "...isn't Dante. I know that much."

"Didn't you get a good look at his face?"

Logan's mouth flattened to a grim line. "Yes, but it's...hard to tell. He was wounded badly."

She closed her eyes briefly against the sudden image that slammed into her thoughts. "Did a—a bear get to the body?"

"No. I think it was a shotgun, close range. Probably more than once. The EMTs agree."

An uneasy feeling turned her blood to ice. "I need to see him, Logan."

"Don't, Carrie. Just wait for the sheriff...and a positive ID."

She started toward the scene, but he gently caught her arm. "This isn't anything you want to remember, Carrie. Believe me."

She shivered at the subtext of his words. "I can't

explain it, but I have a really uneasy feeling about this."

"You and me both." An unreadable expression crossed Logan's face. "And unfortunately, I have a good idea about how all of this is going to go down."

"I need to see him, Logan. Please."

He led her back through the trees to where the two EMTs were kneeling by the blanket-covered body. One of them, a middle-aged man with Phil embroidered on his pocket, was talking on a cell phone. Given the medical jargon he was using, he was probably talking to a physician.

"This is Carrie Randall," Logan said. "She's renting the apartment here and has had some problems with prowlers. She'd like to see the victim."

The two EMTs exchanged glances, and then Phil shoved his cell phone into a holster on his belt and shrugged. His partner, a brunette with Maura emblazoned on her uniform, frowned. "Why?"

"She feels she may know the victim."

Maura shook her head slightly. "Why don't you wait, ma'am. The body will be cleaned up at the funeral home in town. It…won't be quite as difficult, then."

Anxiety roiled through Carrie's stomach. "Please—I just need to know."

Phil lifted back a corner of the blanket.

She'd somehow guessed, even before this moment. A hint of intuition. A sixth sense. A heavy sensation in her heart. Or perhaps just logic, because of Billy's arrival in town and his threats.

Still, disbelief and horror swamped her as she stared down at the remnants of an all-too-familiar face. She could still see the scar traversing what was left of his cheekbone. The thin, cruel twist of the mouth, even in death.

"Billy," she whispered with a hand over her mouth. No wonder Logan had tried to protect her from this.

The world narrowed, the edges of her vision fading to a long, dark tunnel as a loud buzzing sounded in her ears.

And then everything went black.

Three patrol cars arrived one after another, lights flashing. Maura sat with her arm around Carrie on a nearby log. Wrapped in a blanket now, Carrie's head was bowed. She hadn't said a word since she came to after collapsing at the sight of her ex-husband's body.

Logan stood near the body with the EMTs, his arms folded across his chest and his heart heavy as deputies Rick Peterson—as starched and pressed as ever—and Vance Munson climbed out of their vehicles and strode up to the scene.

A moment later the door of the patrol car emblazoned with County Sheriff swung open. His belly wedged behind the steering wheel, Bryce Tyler awkwardly shifted his bulk out of the car and limped to the crime scene, scowling as he favored his left hip.

Logan could see it in the officers' eyes already. The doubt. The judgment. An air of vindication, even. He didn't have to guess that he'd soon feel the cold, hard clamp of handcuffs on his wrists, or that he'd be shoved roughly into the backseat of one of those patrol cars.

They thought he'd gotten away with murder once before, and now they'd do everything in their power to see it didn't happen again. The thick, clotted blood on his hands and shirt would be evidence enough to arrest him.

Phil stepped aside as the sheriff hunkered down to lift away the blanket to study the victim's face. "A group of female customers discovered the body," he murmured. "They arrived early, and were walking through the woods looking for wildflowers."

Tyler's eyes narrowed. "Where are they now?"

"Up at the office, with Penny. One of them was nearly hysterical."

"What did you see when you arrived?"

Phil canted his head toward Logan. "He was performing chest compressions, but it was too late. The guy was gone."

Tyler frowned. "I didn't think you could pronounce a death."

"Not in this county. But we worked on the victim for a good thirty minutes, as well, and maintained communication with the E.R. doctor at Granite Falls

Memorial. This guy was shot at least once. Probably a second time after he was on the ground. He sustained significant blood loss. He was turning cool and gray. Since the pupils were fixed and dilated, and there were no respirations or pulse, we received orders to cease our chest compression efforts." Phil gave him a steady look. "We were also told to leave him exactly as he lay, as it would be a crime scene. As if we didn't know."

Tyler's gaze slid sharply toward Logan, then back to the EMTs. "So the other witnesses have been in the office together, all this time. Was Logan ever up there with them?"

Phil's eyebrows drew together. "No. He was here with Maura and me. Why?"

The sheriff angled a quick glance at Logan—checking for guilt or fear, no doubt.

Logan gave him a steady look in return. "I was doing what I could, hoping to save this guy."

"Right. Vance—I want you to get up to the office. Each one of those tourists needs to be questioned thoroughly, before they have any more time to talk with each other."

"Absolutely, boss." Vance loosened the top button of his rumpled uniform shirt. "I'll get right on it."

"And I want them separated—especially from Penny."

Vance ambled away in the direction of the rafting office. "Sure enough."

"Penny?" Logan straightened. "She's been

nothing but helpful. She's the one who made the 911 call, and—"

"And she's your sister, cowboy," Tyler shot back, flipping open his cell phone and hitting a single digit. He spoke rapidly into the phone, then snapped it shut and shoved it into his breast pocket.

Rick's cold gaze darted between Logan and Carrie, who was still leaning over her folded arms. "Was that the BCI on the phone?"

The sheriff nodded. "They've got a crime unit wrapping up a murder scene just over the county line. They'll have a couple men here within an hour, and the rest of the team and a mobile lab will be here within two. We'll process the scene while we wait, then let them have at it."

Logan sighed under his breath. The arrival of the Montana Bureau of Criminal Investigation meant the investigation would be handled right...*unless* the local department managed to destroy the evidence first through sheer incompetence, if not intent. They'd probably already decided he was involved and were just waiting to find proof.

The sheriff turned back to the body and slowly pulled back the blanket, revealing a tangled, blood-soaked shirt. A silver rodeo belt buckle. Faded, muddied jeans.

He lumbered back to his feet, pulled a digital camera from the bag at his side and began snapping off dozens of shots from every angle. "I've never seen this guy before. Did you find any ID? Was his wallet stolen?"

"It wasn't in any of his pockets." Phil peeled off his vinyl gloves and folded them into each other in one swift motion.

"Well, the BCI's got the lab, ballistics and man-power to cover more ground than we can. From the looks of him, he must have been running through the brush, so maybe his billfold is somewhere in the woods." Tyler pinned Logan with a searching look. "So what do you want to tell us about all of this, Bradley?"

"Maybe the shooter stole it," Logan said slowly. "That would make sense."

"Would it, now. Did you know the victim?"

"I think I saw him briefly for the first time Wednesday night, though it was too dark and things happened too fast for a positive ID."

Tyler gave a derisive snort. "Then how would you recognize him now?"

"I'm almost sure." Logan hesitated, regretting the need to involve Carrie, but there was no way out of it. He sent her an apologetic glance. "Carrie says she can positively identify the body, though. She lives out here, and rents the second-floor apartment of the rafting office."

"Carrie?"

"Carrie Randall."

The sheriff shifted his gaze to her. "Why didn't you speak up in the first place? So who is this?"

Carrie lifted her head, the expression in her eyes still shell-shocked, her voice faint. "B-Billy Danvers. My ex-husband."

Rick drew in a sharp breath. "She already told both Vance and me that this guy was a bad one, clear back when she first moved to Granite Falls. She was afraid of him following her here. She'd even filed a restraining order against him."

Tyler's eyes narrowed on her. "You don't say."

"Vance said he responded to a call in town Wednesday night, though it was dark and Danvers melted into the shadows when he arrived," Rick added. "Vance didn't get a look at his face. Ms. Randall, Logan and Danvers were involved in some sort of verbal altercation."

"Now isn't that interesting," the sheriff drawled. "So there's some troubled history, then."

Carrie's eyes widened at the implication. "I had no reason to do him harm, Sheriff."

Rick flipped through the notebook in his hand. "I was out here the second of June on a 911 call because Ms. Randall reported a prowler. She does have a shotgun—I saw it myself. She told me that she'd owned it for years and that she knew how to use it."

So they were already figuring she had both motive and means…and out in the dark pine forest, they'd assume that there would have been plenty of opportunity. But there wouldn't be evidence. There *couldn't* be. "It—it's hardly uncommon to own a weapon if you've grown up on a ranch."

She appeared so pale and fragile. No wonder, after what she'd just seen, and now the two officers seemed as intent as terriers after a rabbit. As if they thought they could close the case in the next few hours and get back home for a good night's sleep.

The sheriff and his deputy exchanged looks. "Where is that shotgun now?"

"It's in my a-apartment. But I haven't used it for a good six months or more."

"So you'd have it handy in case your ex-husband showed up, I take it. Did he threaten you, Ms. Randall?"

"I had put it in the back of my SUV when I moved to Granite Falls. When Deputy Peterson was out here, he insisted that I bring it up to the apartment so I'd have some protection. It's on the top shelf of my bedroom closet."

"Rick—go get it and tag it as evidence. The BCI can run the ballistics."

"Yes, sir."

"But it hasn't been loaded in *months*," Carrie protested, her face pale.

"Right."

"But—"

"We'll check it out, ma'am."

"You won't find any connection—I can promise you that."

Tyler arrowed an impatient look back at Rick. "Go."

Rick hesitated. "Another thing you should know... Ranger went crazy inside the cruiser the night I was here on the prowler call."

"Did you let him work the area?"

"I got called out to that fatal accident on the highway. I had to leave."

"So something might've been going on out here even then." The sheriff ground out his words, his eyes narrowed on Carrie, then he swept Logan with a satisfied look, a faint smile curled the edges of his lips. "My men and I need to process this scene, but after that, the three of us are going to have a long, long talk. So don't even *think* about going anywhere. Understood?"

"Are you saying we're under arrest?" Logan stared at the man.

Not one thing could prove he'd had anything to do with the victim's death, yet the sheriff immediately assumed the worst. *Small-town law enforcement in Granite Falls—the easy way out, every single time.*

"Let's just say that you are both 'persons of interest' and that I'm guessing you two might have some valuable information to share." Sheriff Tyler tipped his head toward Rick. "Go get that shotgun and tag it, then come back and settle these two in the backseats of separate patrol cars so there's no more time for any collaboration on details. I'm really looking forward to what each of them has to say."

Rick jogged over to the raft company office, climbed the outside staircase, and went into Carrie's apartment. Ten interminable minutes later he returned with a grim expression.

"I know she owns a shotgun. She admitted it was hers, and I saw it myself. But I just searched every corner of that place and only found an empty box of shells."

Sheriff Tyler turned to stare at her, his eyes cold and suspicious. "Where's that shotgun, Ms. Randall?"

"On my shelf. Like always."

"Well, I've got an officer who says it isn't, and now we have to wonder. What was it used for, and where is it now?"

Still numb with shock and horror, Carrie stepped out of the sheriff's office four hours later. Billy was *dead*.

Any love between them had dissolved long before the divorce. It had then descended to outright animosity on his part, though she'd felt only a cold, empty place in her heart that grew every time he turned up again to rail at her about the settlement and how she "owed" him.

But still…there had been love, once. She'd been excited about becoming his bride. Happy about their future together. And now, he was dead, and she couldn't erase the image of his mangled, bloodied face from her mind.

Having to wait alone, trapped in the backseat of that patrol car until the sheriff was ready to head for town, had escalated her fear until she'd been shaking.

Now, she stood on the sidewalk, too dazed to even think through how she could get home.

"Carrie—over here." Penny stood in front of the Wolf River Rafting Company pickup, just a few parking spaces down. "Need a lift?"

It took a moment for the words to register, then Carrie blinked back tears of relief at seeing a friendly, understanding face after hours of rapid-fire questioning.

Bryce Tyler was a small-town sheriff, but he was no laid-back Andy of Mayberry. He'd acted like a pit bull, sure he could trip her up if he hammered the questions at her long enough, refusing to give up, his face changing to a deeper shade of red as the minutes ticked by.

"What a terrible day." Penny gave her a quick hug. "I'll bet you can't wait to just go home and pull the covers over your head. And for what it's worth, I'm really sorry about your loss. I know it had to be terrible seeing Billy like that…even if you two did have a world of trouble between you."

Carrie drew in a shuddering breath. "We've been apart a long time. I never would've gone back to him. But I never wished him harm. And to die like that… Who would do such a thing? Who would even know him around here?"

"Good question."

"And my shotgun was stolen. Maybe ballistics tests could have proven that it wasn't the one used to kill Billy." She thought a moment. "Or maybe the killer actually used it—so it would look like I killed him and hid the weapon."

"Or that Logan did," Penny said bitterly.

"Is he with you?"

"He's already home. I came after him over an hour ago." Penny climbed behind the wheel of the truck, fastened her seat belt, and waited until Carrie was inside before starting the engine. "Our good sheriff grilled him, too, but fortunately he had an alibi."

Carrie frowned. "I assumed he stayed in the boat-house last night, but no one questioned me about it."

"He was going to, but Aunt Betty and I called him at ten last night. She had a water pipe break and her place flooded. The three of us worked on it through the wee hours, until Logan and I had to get back to set up for our breakfast float group. You had the dog, though…and since your lights were out, he didn't call to tell you when he left for Betty's place."

"Thank goodness he can prove he wasn't near the murder scene."

"As long as they believe Aunt Betty and me, anyway."

"From what I hear about the sheriff, the phrase 'innocent until proven guilty' doesn't seem to be part of his code." Carrie bent over her clasped hands, feeling more exhausted than she ever had in her life, her stomach still roiling.

"Never has been. I think it's more in line with 'take the easy way out' and go with the first suspect you see."

"But the scary part is that I can understand why I'd be a suspect. Too many witnesses saw that confrontation with Billy after the movie, and both deputies were aware of the problems I'd had with him in the past. In their shoes, I guess I'd feel the same."

"Though you'd probably do a better job of investigating. I just hope this doesn't end up like last year." Penny gripped the steering wheel until her knuckles turned white. "Logan was just a casual friend of Sheryl Colwell, even if several witnesses placed him close to the crime scene and one claimed the two of them had had an affair. The sheriff should've known perfectly well that Logan wasn't guilty, yet he had to go through an entire trial."

Carrie felt an icy hand clamp down on her insides. "You hear all the time about falsely accused people going to jail for years and years."

"Luckily, in his case the jury was fair and didn't believe the circumstantial evidence."

"Yet some folks still think he's guilty."

"He was judged innocent because he didn't do it, plain and simple, not because of some failure in the legal system. But people believe what they want to believe, I guess."

"Still, now that Logan and I have been questioned, we should be free and clear."

"In an ideal world. But frankly, I don't think this is over." Penny backed out of the parking space and headed out of town. "I'm not a betting woman, but if I were, I'd bet that the sheriff is hoping to charge one of you—or both, and say you plotted to get rid of your ex-husband. He probably already thinks you hired Logan to help you once you learned of his past history."

"But…your brother has witnesses saying he couldn't have been there."

"You think that's enough?" Penny said bitterly. "His 'witnesses' are his great-aunt and his sister. The right prosecuting attorney can practically make a jury believe the sun rises at dusk…and discredit the best defense." She pulled to a stop at the four-way flashing red light on Main and Fourth, then drove on. "You know what? I even wonder if Billy was killed close by, just to set Logan up."

Carrie's stomach tied itself into a painful knot.

"And now you're mixed up in this, too. I'm just going to start praying that the state investigators come up with better answers than our sheriff's department will, or my brother will never truly be free. And now, neither will you. My biggest question is this—since Logan isn't a killer, then who has tried to frame him *twice?*"

ELEVEN

She'd been questioned for hours on Sunday, then returned home to find a large van and several dark sedans parked close to the murder site. The investigators from the BCI talked to her at length, as well, showing marked interest in the recent emails Billy had sent, the history of their troubled marriage, and the prowler who'd been in the area.

By Monday morning the numbness and shock began to wear off and the true horror of it all felt like a cold, hard anvil weighing down her heart. Billy, for all his faults, had charmed her once. She'd loved him back then, and there *had* been good times. The thought of his brutal murder—of his lifeless body and the unbelievable amount of blood at the scene—made her stomach pitch and her eyes burn.

On the verge of tears during a long, sleepless night, she debated calling in sick, then resolutely dressed and turned up for work anyway, figuring it would feel better to be occupied and surrounded by people than to sit at home with her dark thoughts.

Appearing uncharacteristically sympathetic, Mr. Grover appeared at her door halfway through the morning and beckoned her out into the hallway.

"I heard about what happened at your place," he said solemnly. "I'm sorry to hear about your loss. The victim was your ex-husband, I hear."

She nodded.

"Obviously suspicious circumstances."

She swallowed hard, trying to clear the sudden lump in her throat. "Yes."

"The BCI has been asking questions of us here. So has the sheriff."

The lump in her throat turned to granite. "Questions?"

"About your character. Suspicious activities. That sort of thing."

She stared at the principal, unable to form any words. She already knew the investigators had an interest in her. It made sense, given the history between Billy and her, but after all the questioning over the weekend she'd assumed they now believed in her innocence and would be looking for other suspects.

Apparently not.

"I just wanted you to know that we've had nothing negative to say," the principal continued. "As far as we know, you appear to have good rapport with the students, and care a lot about them."

"Thank you."

His smiled faintly. "I'm sure they're questioning

a lot of people, though, trying to figure out what happened that night."

She nodded. "I just wish Billy had never come here. He'd still be alive. And I wish they'd hurry and find the killer. What if he strikes again?"

"As you can imagine, the people around here are plenty nervous. We even had some families call in this morning to say they were keeping their kids at home today."

"Three are missing in my class."

He eyed her closely. "So how are you holding up? If you want to leave early, I can take over for the last two hours. And if you need a few days— even weeks—off, I'm sure we can arrange it. No trouble—no trouble at all."

"I'm…I'm okay."

"Have the kids given you any problems?"

"I figured the Nelson twins would have a lot of questions, at the very least. But all of the kids are… well, subdued. Maybe even a little frightened, thinking about what happened so close to where they all live. I'm keeping them busy with mixed-media sculptures."

"Good, good." Mr. Grover straightened his tie. "Well, then, I'll leave you to it. But if you change your mind, just give me a call—or call my secretary. Dottie will arrange things."

His hearty manner and air of concern had fooled her at first, but as he strode away, the subtext of his visit sank in.

He'd been hoping she'd take time off. He didn't want her here. Small matters, in the face of Billy's tragic death, but once again, her future in Granite Falls might be on the line.

On Wednesday evening, after her last white-water rafting certification class, Carrie headed into town for some groceries. Between her mornings at the school followed by the river classes and several more long meetings with various investigators, the time marched by, inexorably slow, while questions and worries swirled through her thoughts.

And it wasn't only her who had questions.

She'd seen them in the eyes of the other teachers. On the faces of her silent, subdued students…and in the growing number of empty desks in her classroom.

Without a prisoner behind bars, the murder just outside of Granite Falls had to be the biggest topic in anyone's mind…and she had no doubt about what they were saying behind closed doors.

Now, standing in the checkout line at the town's only grocery store, she could feel the stares of the other customers passing by and make out some of the whispers. *"That's her. And he was killed just a few hundred yards from her apartment."*

Norma was at the cash register. She met Carrie's eyes briefly and nodded, then turned her attention back to a two-cart load of groceries belonging to a hefty woman with four young children clambering for treats from the candy display by the register.

When it was finally Carrie's turn, Norma leaned over the counter and grasped her hand in a quick squeeze. "How are things going, hon?"

Warmed by her concern, Carrie dipped her head and sighed. "Pretty well, I guess."

"A big mess, I'd say. This whole town is on edge, worrying about who committed that murder. I hear they don't even have a clue so far."

"Which is probably why they keep talking to me. But I didn't know much about Billy's life anymore, so I'm not much help."

"Sheriff came in this morning with his picture, asking if any of us had seen him around town. Handsome fella."

"Too handsome for his own good, probably. He… liked to party way too much."

She clucked her tongue. "I still can't say if he was the one asking about you soon after you moved here. Barely caught a glimpse of the guy's face, and that's what I told the sheriff, all right. Worries me, though, that someone would come into town all sneaky like, wanting to find out where a woman lives. No good could come of that."

Amen. "So…you never saw that guy again?"

Norma flicked a glance at a customer who'd just wheeled a cart into line behind Carrie, then leaned closer. "Not that I know of. But I have a real bad feeling about all of this."

"No kidding."

"I don't think it was some random thing at all, like the sheriff said in the paper this morning. If the killer was just someone who drifted through, that would make no sense. At least, that's what they say on those *Law & Order* reruns. The bad guy is often someone the victim knows." She worried at her lower lip with her front teeth, then lowered her voice. "I heard some details from my cousin Edna, who works down at the mortuary part-time as the evening receptionist. She said someone must've had a real passion about getting the job done, with no chance of survival. He also had to be pretty close. So you've gotta think it was someone your husband knew—someone he trusted. Otherwise, a big man like Billy could've put up a big fight and he would've had a lot of bruises. And he didn't."

Small-town gossips, Carrie thought grimly. No secrets were ever safe. What else did the cops know that they weren't sharing? "You're right."

"My niece is in your morning class—Rachel— and she likes you a whole lot. I'd listen to what's in her heart before I'd listen to the cops any day." A smile flickered briefly on Norma's face, though it didn't touch the sadness in her eyes. "We need people in town like you. Like a breath of fresh air. I'll be prayin' for you every night, hon. I promise you that."

On Monday, Noah had been marked absent. "Just a flu bug," the school secretary had reassured her when Carrie used the intercom to check with the office. But he wasn't in school on Tuesday, Wednesday or Thursday, either. And not one new drawing of violence appeared in his absence.

On Friday, Carrie unlocked her desk when she arrived and found her folder of the mysterious drawings was gone.

She drew in a sharp breath. Searched all of the drawers, the stacks of papers on her desk and her briefcase. Who could've taken it, and *why?*

A second, closer inspection of the drawer that had held the missing folder yielded a single drawing— the newest version—that had slipped beneath some other papers.

She slid it into her purse, put it in the file cabinet behind her desk and locked the drawer.

As soon as her class was over, she hurried across the hall to Marie's room. "I already had a strong suspicion, but I now know who did those drawings."

Marie glanced up, then continued sorting a box of pieces that appeared to be from an old Erector Set. "Really."

"Noah has been gone all week, and not one picture has appeared during his absence."

"Good guess, then."

Carrie stared at her. "I was already pretty sure. But you knew all along?"

Marie shrugged. "Let's just say it wouldn't surprise me."

"And now the folder of drawings has disappeared

from a locked desk in my room." She caught the uncertainty in the older woman's eyes. "Do you know about that, as well?"

Marie turned away, ostensibly to straighten the supplies on her desk. "Just let it go."

"This child seems incredibly quiet. Disconnected. I know he must be grieving badly over his mother, and I wonder just how much counseling and support he's really getting." At Marie's sharp glance, Carrie fell silent for a long moment. "I should have been told about things like this before the very first class this summer. Noah should be receiving extra help."

"We don't have resources in this district for extra services. Just do some research on children and grief. It takes time for anyone. And if you've met his family, you know that his father and aunt are very protective of him. Noah—for the most part—has done fine. I'm sure he's moving beyond that unfortunate tragedy and is simply back to his normal, quiet self."

Unfortunate tragedy? Carrie's mouth dropped open at the sheer insensitivity of the woman's remarks. "Then what about all the violent pictures he draws? With a river that flows red with blood? That doesn't seem like the hallmark of a well-adjusted child to me."

"What do you expect, after what happened in his life?" Marie taped the top of the cardboard box shut and turned to set it on a shelf in her supply closet.

"He was in Miss Carson's class last year. He was really troubled for the first half of the year, but he was seen by the school counselor once a month. By spring he started to do much better."

Only once a month? "If he's doing so well, why hasn't he been in class all week?"

Marie glanced at the doorway, then raised an eyebrow when she looked back at Carrie. "Uh… he's not the only kid who isn't in school now. A lot of people are worried about their safety these days. Maybe you want to talk to Mr. Grover about this."

Carrie turned toward the door to find the principal frowning at her. "I'm just worried, that's all."

He beckoned her out into the hallway. "As I said before, I understand that you're new here."

"But not new to teaching. And I'm—"

"Concerned. I understand that as well, and I'm trying very hard to be patient with you and with… with that other situation. But the resources you might have seen in a big-city classroom aren't exactly what we can offer children here. In many ways I think the more intimate, caring educational setting of a small town can offer more. Would you agree it's possible?"

"Well, yes, but—"

"Ms. Randall. The teachers here know the kids practically from birth. There's continuity here because staff turnover is rare, and they see the kids growing up throughout their school years, along with their siblings and cousins and neighbors. Our kids do well on the basic skills tests and college entrance exams. And because our student population is small, a child like Noah does not fall through the cracks."

Carrie sighed. "I understand."

"We *are* open to new teaching philosophies, but we believe in solid tradition, as well. You can rest assured that he is receiving the consistency and quality of education that he needs until he is successfully launched toward college, trade school or whatever else he dreams of." His bushy silver eyebrows drew together. "We do well with our tight budget, and will continue to do so—even with the very big cuts we're facing next fall."

He must have given this very speech before, and his words were logical and calm, delivered with an edge that made his true meaning clear. The system was entrenched. And no crusading, upstart teacher was going to rock the boat and still find herself still employed.

"I understand," she repeated, disappointment washing through her.

"Good, good." He glanced at his watch. "Now I'm late. Afternoon, ladies."

Carrie watched him bustle down the hall toward the exit. "That was sure helpful."

"I tried to tell you," Marie said, joining her at the doorway. "This is one principal who is all about the status quo. Me? Maybe I started out with stars in my eyes, but I don't want to move away. Now I'm just happy doing the best job I can within the system, and I let it go at that."

"This isn't what I want." Carrie reined in her frustration. "But it's way too late to look elsewhere for the fall and I *need* a job to pay off my legal expenses from the divorce."

"You also wouldn't want the bad reference you'd get if you broke your contract for the fall. And given that other little problem of yours, I can't think of a school system that would want to take a chance. At least, until the murder investigation is over."

"But shouldn't the welfare of a child matter more than anything?"

"Absolutely." Marie rested her hand on Carrie's arm. "You can help Noah a great deal, when he comes back. Just like his teacher did all last year with consistency and attention and praise."

"I guess."

"So, do you have time for lunch today?"

All of the other teachers had been distant since the weekend of Billy's death, and though Marie had remained cordial, this was the first real gesture of friendship anyone at the school had offered since Billy died. "I'd like to, but I work at the raft office this afternoon."

"So you're still getting along okay out there?"

"It's quiet, but fine." Carrie sighed. "Business is slow."

Marie shuddered. "Well, I'll have to say that you're a braver woman than I am, just for staying out there. No matter what people say, I don't believe you could've had anything to do with murder. And I'd always be wondering—what if the killer comes back?"

TWELVE

On Friday, a week after Principal Grover's sharp words in the hall outside her classroom, Noah still hadn't come back to summer school. He and his aunt hadn't been in church, either.

So when Carrie saw them outside the tiny town library on Monday afternoon, she hesitated, then pulled her Tahoe into an empty parking space a half block away and walked back.

Noah saw her first and offered a tentative smile of welcome. But when his aunt glanced around to follow his gaze, she stiffened and grabbed his hand.

"Hi, there," Carrie said warmly, smiling at them both. "Beautiful summer day, isn't it?"

Noah's smile wobbled, then faded when his aunt gave his hand a slight jerk of warning. "Yes, it is," she said. She shoved a long hank of dishwater-blond hair behind her eye. "So I guess we'd better be going."

She turned to leave and Noah obediently followed,

though he glanced over his shoulder at Carrie as if he wanted to say something but didn't dare. "I hope we'll get to see Noah back at school someday," she called out.

Linda continued on a few more strides, but slowed to a stop, her shoulders slumped. She whispered a few words to Noah and gestured toward a bench in front of the bank, waiting until he dutifully went to the bench and sat down, and then she turned back.

Carrie expected to face the woman's anger over whatever issue had precipitated Noah's withdrawal from summer school. The look of defeat in Linda's eyes caught her off guard. "I'm so glad to see you two. I've missed Noah in class."

Linda's gaze darted protectively toward the boy, then skated back to Carrie. "Well, he won't be back. Not this summer, anyway."

"But—"

"Please, just drop it. I— It isn't possible."

"I only want to help," Carrie said softly.

Linda swallowed hard. "His father has done everything he can to shelter Noah after what he's been through. Undue attention just makes things worse."

"I didn't mean to—"

"But it happened. And it was all I could do to convince David to stay in Granite Falls, and let Noah come back to school here in the fall. He thinks his son needs a fresh start elsewhere, where no one knows about Sheryl's death and no one will ever bring it up. I think Noah needs familiar surroundings, but I'm not the one to decide." She glanced again at the boy, and lowered her voice. "Look, his father and I do know about the pictures he draws. He's done them at home—many of them. The counselor says he's trying to deal with his mother's death this way. We're keeping him close to home for the rest of the summer, where he can feel safe with the last two people he has left in this world. Understand?"

"I can only imagine how hard this has been for all of you. If there's anything I can do, just say the word."

"What you can do is just leave us alone. Don't be telling people about his drawings and how troubled he is. Understand? I know he's got problems. His father and I are dealing with them, best we can." She closed her eyes briefly, then continued in a lower tone. "When you talked to the principal, he had his secretary contact us. We don't want Noah labeled as being 'disturbed,' understand?"

"But I didn't—"

"It's all the same, if people talk about his 'crazy pictures.' Dottie is one of the biggest gossips in town, and now that could happen."

"I'm sorry."

"Everyone knows about Sheryl's murder. They don't need to make Noah an object of pity or curiosity."

"Honestly, I didn't know they were Noah's drawings, until that day. I was just worried about the child who'd anonymously left them for me. I thought it might just be the usual stuff fifth-grade boys like to draw, yet…"

"Look, Noah still has nightmares. He wakes up screaming several times a week. Sometimes he awakens and cries into his pillow for his mom, trying to avoid waking up my brother and me. During the day, it's better. But…well, the counselors say it will just take a long time." Linda glanced down the street and shifted uneasily. "He was *mortified* when you asked the class who might have drawn those pictures. So just leave us alone. You've done enough damage as it is."

Logan helped the last Girl Scout out of the raft, then pulled it higher up the bank and took off his life jacket and tossed it back in the raft.

By the time he turned back to group, Carrie had already emerged from the office and was helping the girls and their leaders with their own life jackets.

She was dressed in a pretty pink top and khaki shorts today, colors that emphasized her deepening tan. He needed to stop noticing what she wore and how she looked.

Since he'd told her about competing in rodeos, there had been a wall of ice between them that time was never going to melt. And that was just as well.

He'd be leaving in a few weeks—unless the murder investigation forced him to stay—and wouldn't be back for six months. Even if the impossible occurred and she deigned to give him the time of day, he already knew how well long-distance relationships worked. Not at all.

When the last girl climbed back on the shuttle bus, Carrie dusted off her hands. "Nice group."

"Sharper than the last group of adults Tina took down the river. Did she tell you about them?"

Carrie's pretty bow of a mouth tipped up briefly. "I believe that was the group with the lady who asked about when Montana's deer molted and turned into elk."

He laughed. "I just want to know how Tina handled that one. I think I would have lost it, right then and there."

"City folks." She grabbed an armload of life jackets and wrestled them into the boathouse, where she began hanging them on a row of pegs by size.

He grabbed the last three and followed her. "You don't seem as chipper as usual. Is something wrong?"

She settled the last life jacket into place. "No."

"There is, too." He cracked a smile. "Was someone rude on the phone?"

"No."

"Impatient to start guiding on the river? As soon as things get busier we'll be sure to get you on the schedule."

"I look forward to that, now that I've finished those certification classes. But that's not it."

He thought for a minute. "You have second thoughts about your afternoon job here?"

"No. The first two weeks have been fine. No complaints." She turned and leaned against the wall. "I just had an encounter with a student's family member after school today, and discovered that I've inadvertently made things a thousand times worse for that child." Carrie sighed. "With the best intentions, but still…"

"I can't believe that."

"Do."

"Can you tell me about it?"

She gave him a bleak glance. "Nope."

"You look like you need cheering up. Want to go out on the river? We could take one of the two-man rafts. Or Penny could go, when she gets back."

"That's sweet of you to offer. But I'm sure it's the last thing you two would want to do after being on the water all day."

"Take a kayak or a canoe then, if you'd rather go solo. Sometimes things just look better when you can get out and do something."

She stilled for a moment, then shook her head. "It's already five o'clock, and I have papers to grade. But thanks—maybe another time."

He smiled gently. "I know you've got an awful lot on your mind. But things will work out."

"Easy for you to say." She tried to dredge up an

answering grin. "You didn't just put your foot in your mouth."

"I can't imagine you ever doing that." He surveyed the long row of life jackets on the wall, straightened one, then picked up a yellow kayak and settled it on a triple-stack kayak rack in the corner. He turned to face her. "Just so you know, Penny and I have been asking a lot of questions around town. And sooner or later, the man who killed Billy *will* be found. I can promise you that."

Wednesday morning dawned way too early, after yet another sleepless night, with heavy fog blanketing the lower half of the mountains and a chilly mist that jeweled the pines in diamonds. If the forecasters were right, rain would be moving into the area by midmorning and then linger for much of the day, meaning few customers would be signing up for rafting today and most of the reservations would be cancelled.

Not that there'd been many in the first place, according to Penny.

At school, only half of the students showed up, so Carrie postponed her lesson on a comparison of Mayan and American Indian art, and let them get started on a pottery project. She strolled back and forth between the tables, offering advice and praise, and keeping an eye on the Nelson boys, who lobbed missiles of clay at each other from either side of the room whenever her back was turned.

She smiled to herself at the consternation of the twins and the awe of the others, who were all apparently unaware of the lovely, reflective properties of the framed map of America to the left of the blackboard.

Austin zinged a piece of clay at Rachel, then played innocent when Carrie whirled around to glare at him.

Fifth graders. On the cusp of starting to notice the opposite sex, but most were nowhere close to understanding or caring about the subtleties of an actual relationship.

"Austin, that's enough. If you can't handle this project with the others, perhaps you need to sit way in the back, and face the windows."

Austin slipped down in his seat, the tips of his ears bright red.

"Ms. Randall." Ed Grover stood in the doorway, frowning. "Can you come here for a minute?"

If she'd been sitting, she might have wanted to slide down in her seat, too. "Keep at it, class." She gave Austin a stern look. "I'll be just outside the door."

The principal ushered her out into the hallway and closed the door. "I just learned that Noah Colwell won't be back in school for the rest of the summer."

"That's correct. He—"

"His aunt says he was uncomfortable in class, and didn't want to return. Is that true?"

"Yes…she wants to keep him home and—"

"Ms. Randall. This hasn't been an auspicious start for you here." He rocked back on his heels. "We're not even halfway through summer school and several students in your class have dropped out. We *need* our students. Every last one of them. I'm especially concerned when a troubled child like Noah—who's in need of our help—drops out. We've let him down, don't you think?"

She felt a sinking sensation in the pit of her stomach at hearing him echo her own feelings. "Unintentionally."

"What if she decides to homeschool, or something? Then we've lost state funding, and in a district this size, we need every child we can get."

Homeschooling could be a wonderful option, when parents were dedicated. Children often ended ahead of their public school counterparts when they received such individualized attention, and she'd often thought she'd try it herself if she ever got her life straightened out and had a family. But from the tone in his voice, Grover probably didn't want to hear *that*. He seemed more concerned with funding than the child himself.

"Pay his aunt a visit," he continued. "Apologize for whatever it was that upset the kid. See if you can get him back."

"I just saw them in town on Monday. I don't think—"

"You aren't paid to do that. It's my job."

Ouch. His words rasped against her skin like rough sandpaper. "I did try to talk with Linda. She feels he just needs time to get over his loss, and Mr. Colwell feels the same."

The principal glowered at her. "You can try again, right?"

Carrie sighed. "Of course, if you want me to go talk to them, I'll be happy to do so."

"Good, good. Let me know how it goes." He pursed his lips as he gave her a long, assessing look. "I have a feeling that you can smooth the waters with them both, if you put your mind to it."

She watched him stride down the hall, and once again, she had the feeling that her future in the Granite Falls school system was hanging in the balance. But where did the true importance lie?

It wasn't her own future that mattered most. She would go talk to Linda Bates and her brother to discuss Noah's best interests...and just pray that she could make everyone happy.

THIRTEEN

It was raining by noon. The students all grumbled as they left school to walk home in the rain or went to wait for their parents at the front entrance, but Carrie savored the wonderfully drippy weather as she walked to her Tahoe under her bright red umbrella. She'd always loved rain.

Penny had already texted her to say that there'd be no need to work this afternoon, so after she finished her visit with Linda and Mr. Colwell at Noah's house, she'd drop by one of the quaint coffee shops in town or maybe even head for the bookstore over in Battle Creek—rainy weather was perfect for curling up with a good book and a hot cup of tea. Maybe she'd even stop in to see Trace and Kris, though she'd have to watch the time. Rain, nightfall and mountain roads were a combination she tried to avoid.

She drove slowly through town, past the gift shops and high-adventure sporting goods shops, the little touristy restaurants and small artisans' galleries.

At the end of town she glanced again at the map and directions she'd printed off the internet, then continued on for several miles until the signs for Granite Peak and Wilderness Park came into view. A right turn took her up a narrow, winding road that turned from asphalt to gravel at the four-mile point, where it grew even steeper and passed several rustic, tumbledown cabins that obviously hadn't been used for years.

The fourth one was the oldest, its logs weathered and gray, and the car parked in front had seen better days. Still, the yard was neatly kept and the windows shone. Carrie pulled up next to the car and climbed from behind her wheel, unfurled her umbrella and trotted up to the door.

It opened before she made it to the top step.

"What are you doing here?" Linda whispered. She glanced over her shoulder into the cabin then stepped outside, pulling the front door closed. "I already told you that Noah wouldn't be back this summer."

"I understand. But Principal Grover wanted me to make sure everything is all right. Can we talk— maybe with Noah's father, too?"

Linda anxiously surveyed the yard, then her worried gaze flitted back to Carrie. She reached for the doorknob. "My brother is asleep, actually—he got in late last night and has to leave again very early tomorrow morning."

"Is there another time? I can come back."

"He's a long-haul trucker, so he comes and goes to the east and west coast all the time. I can't tell you when he'll be back next—at least until he marks it on the calendar for me."

"Then, can I talk to you?"

"I have nothing to say."

Carrie started to envision her fall teaching contract going up in smoke. "But what about Noah—and school in the fall?"

A door slammed. Heavy footsteps creaked across an uncarpeted floor, drawing closer.

Linda shook her head. "You *really* shouldn't have come."

"I'm only doing my job. I'm sorry if—"

A burly man pulled the front door open wider, his red plaid shirt stretched across his ample belly. Probably in his forties, the dark stubble on his face and the weary expression in his eyes suggested he'd been short of sleep for some time.

"What's going on out here?"

Linda stepped aside. "David, this is Ms. Carrie Randall. She is—or was—Noah's teacher for the summer."

He shoved a hand through his thinning black hair and frowned. "So you're the one. Why are you here?"

"The principal asked me to come for a brief visit, just to talk to you about school in the fall."

His expression darkened. "Frankly, I don't want Noah there at all, though my sister disagrees."

"I still feel so badly about upsetting him, Mr. Colwell. I never meant to do that. Maybe it would help if the three of us could sit down for a talk, so he'd understand why I asked—"

"About his drawings? I handled it."

"But—"

"Just drop it." He folded his heavily muscled arms across his chest. "Honestly, I'd homeschool him if I could, but I'm on the road all the time and Linda dropped out of high school, so she's afraid she doesn't have the experience. I just want him kept away from *anyone* who might upset him. My son has suffered more than any child ever should, from the things people say to him in town."

"I understand. Totally." Carrie debated for a moment. "If you're really interested in homeschooling, I can get you in touch with the local homeschool association. They offer resources and guidance."

"I made my decision. You can tell your principal that Noah will be back. But nothing means more to me than my son. So if he comes home crying again, I'll pull him out faster than you can say goodbye."

He stepped back and shut the door in Carrie's face.

Carrie stared at it for a moment, feeling as if she'd just encroached on enemy territory. Was it so wrong to ask about the child's welfare? Was the man simply being protective, or had he tipped over into paranoia?

Maybe she'd just confirmed the answer Principal

Grover wanted regarding school in the fall, but she sure hadn't managed to establish better rapport.

And until Linda or the boy's father decided to open up—if ever—apparently that was how things were going to stay.

Logan had stayed overnight in the boathouse ever since the murder, and always left Murphy with Carrie in her apartment. The dog seemed to understand the new routine, because he settled down and didn't pace and whine through the night.

On Tuesday afternoon after a long discussion, Logan finally agreed to go back to staying at his cabin…as long as Carrie kept the dog overnight and her cell phone handy.

"So now it'll be just you and me, buddy," Carrie said, stroking the old dog's head as she watched the last customer's car pull out. "But we'll be fine."

Buttoning her sweater against the evening chill, she sauntered over to the boathouse to help Logan and Penny finish putting away the equipment. Murphy followed and curled up on his bed in the corner of the building.

"There were several more calls while you were gone, and four more reservations via the internet. Things are looking good for the next week or so."

"Thanks. It helps to have a voice instead of a recording if people call." Penny smiled. "And that's just the news we want to hear."

Murphy suddenly stood up, his head up and ears

pricked, his tail low and still, then he bolted out of the building to stare at the line of trees to the south, near the river's edge.

Logan motioned for Penny and Carrie to stay inside. "I'll go check around."

They stood in the doorway and watched him go. Dusk was falling, and now the world was in shades of muted gray. In just a few strides Logan disappeared. Carrie wrapped her arms around her middle, straining to see where he'd gone.

Someone else appeared out of the shadows. Voices drifted through the darkness. Logan's tone insistent, the stranger's voice hesitant.

"I think it's Dante Loomis," Penny said, after listening intently.

"You mentioned him once before. Who is he?"

"A reclusive old guy who's lived off the land up in the mountains somewhere since coming back from Vietnam. He doesn't show up for weeks or even months at a time, then drifts into town for supplies—more alcohol, mostly. The younger kids are frightened of him because he looks scary with all that scraggly hair, but he's harmless. He hasn't ever harmed a soul around here, anyway. I hate to think what he might've been through in that war."

"Sounds like a troubled guy."

"Exactly. They say he was normal before. Now, he supposedly has quite an arsenal, is suspicious of everyone and is still convinced that 'government agents' are after him."

"Shouldn't he have gotten help? Like at a veterans' hospital somewhere?"

"You'd think, but he would have none of it. Come on—you should meet him in case you run into him out here sometime. Logan?" Penny called out. "We're coming."

Carrie followed her outside to where Logan and Dante stood at the far end of the parking area, under a pool of light from the security lamp overhead.

She could see why small children might be frightened. A good six feet tall, Dante was dressed in multiple layers of ragged clothes, with an army surplus–style backpack hooked over one arm. Between the long, wispy hair erupting in wild tangles from beneath the old baseball cap pulled low over his eyes and his scraggly beard, he was more apparition than man in the dim light.

One bony hand repeatedly plucked at the buttons of his jacket while his head swiveled back and forth like a radar dish as if he were anxiously scanning the area for the fastest escape route. He gave Carrie a furtive glance, then dropped his gaze and shuffled his feet.

"Dante, this is Carrie. She works for us." Logan spoke distinctly, slowly. "She's a good lady."

"I'm glad to meet you, Dante." Carrie stepped forward and offered her hand, but the man took a wary step backward. "Nice evening, isn't it?"

He craned his head in an odd motion, met her eyes for a split second—probably incredulous because she couldn't have come up with a more inane thing to say—and then he spun on his heel and loped off into the darkness.

"That went well," she muttered, feeling a flush of embarrassment. "I said ten words and sent him running."

Logan chuckled. "Actually, it *did* go well. He hung around long enough to meet you before taking off, and that doesn't always happen...or so we've heard. He's shy as a wild deer around most folks."

She stared into the gloom, trying to make out his retreating form. "I feel sorry for him."

Penny nodded. "Me, too. But we heard that he ran away from several facilities over the years, and refused psych treatment. I guess he's living the life he wants."

Carrie hesitated. "Does he show up around here often?"

"Nope...maybe just two or three times during the two years we've been here. Right, Logan?"

"At the most. And once was just a glimpse."

"Maybe he could've been the prowler I saw."

"Like we said, he doesn't come around here much," Penny said. "He avoids civilization. So the likelihood that you saw him is pretty slim."

"What about Billy's murder? Couldn't he be a suspect?"

"Dante? I doubt it."

"Was he ever questioned?"

"I actually did hear that he was, but not for long. He doesn't always make a lot of sense."

"Even if he didn't do it, maybe he saw something suspicious, if he's been hanging around this area."

Penny and Logan exchanged glances.

"A slim chance, maybe. But like I said, he's a recluse. Even if he claimed he'd seen something and was brought in to testify, I doubt a court of law would believe him," Penny said slowly. "Then again…I suppose anything is possible."

After coming to Granite Falls, Carrie had twice felt the eerie, unseen presence of someone watching her, and she'd seen a prowler once. With the timing of Billy's emails and his ultimate arrival in town, she'd been sure that he was the one who'd been lurking in the shadows. But now, there was an alternate explanation.

It could have been Dante, with his secretive, vagabond ways, though Logan and Penny had both insisted that the old guy was harmless. Maybe he'd just been curious about someone new moving into his territory.

The more frightening possibility was one that she didn't want to think about—that the prowler had been Billy's killer. A killer who was still at large.

Had Billy been a random victim—or a specific target? Knowing her ex-husband, he could've headed north to escape serious gambling debts or a run-in with a dangerous element at some honky-tonk bar.

That could explain why he'd come back to Montana to find her, and wanted money so badly.

If the guy had come after him from down South, maybe he was long gone. If it had been a random act…

She shivered, thinking about the dense forest and the perfect cover it offered. The rushing water of the nearby river that could mask the sound of someone approaching.

Saying a silent prayer to herself, she tried to shove those fears aside as she showered and put on her favorite Snoopy pj's and a red summer-weight cotton sweater, then checked her windows and door locks and whistled to Murphy as she headed for bed.

Watching from the shadows at the end of the boathouse, his frustration grew by the minute.

It had seemed so perfect.

A grisly murder on the Bradley property and Logan's past legal history should have immediately branded him as the lone suspect. Eliminated all future risk and helped settle the past once and for all. Even better, there'd been a perfect victim— one who had been in the wrong place at the wrong time and had inadvertently seen too much. When he became confrontational there'd been no other option but to eliminate him, but there couldn't have been a better choice. Learning that the ex-wife probably had good reason to see Billy disappear had been icing on the cake.

But oh, no.

Despite a murder in his own backyard, Logan had come up with an alibi that would probably hold up in court. And now people were beginning to dredge up the topic of Sheryl Colwell's death again. Starting to think Logan seemed like a "nice young man" and wondering why he'd ever been brought to trial for her murder.

Those questions were dangerous.

Though there'd been no witnesses in either case, questions could lead to more curiosity. And if anyone delved too deeply into Sheryl's past…

Cursing under his breath, the man lifted his gaze to the curtained windows of the apartment above the rafting company office and watched the silhouette of the woman checking her windows and turning off the lights, one by one.

The sheriff was a fool and the BCI investigators clearly weren't much better, but he'd been careful to eliminate evidence at each murder scene at any rate, for he was a meticulous man. But Penny, Logan and Carrie were starting to ask questions around town… and he knew they wouldn't stop until they'd discovered way too much. They had to be stopped.

And if one of them needed to die to make that happen, so be it.

FOURTEEN

Though business had been slow the week before, the July Fourth holiday brought a welcome surge in reservations. Penny and Tina each took groups on six-hour white-water trips, while Logan took care of slow-paced scenic float trips both morning and afternoon. He'd let Carrie guide with him on his early morning run, then she'd guided her first scenic float down the river solo, with a small group of passengers from California.

Now, at eight o'clock in the evening, the customers and Tina were long gone. Logan had just finished grilling hamburgers and brats out next to the river, while Penny and Carrie shook a red-checked tablecloth over the picnic table by the boathouse and brought out potato salad, baked beans and thick wedges of watermelon.

"Gorgeous evening," Carrie said, her voice wistful. "Brings back a lot of memories."

A shadow of worry crossed her expression, and

Logan wondered if she was remembering any good ones spent with her ex-husband.

"What are some of your favorites?" Penny asked as she adjusted the foil covering on a bowl of potato salad that she'd set in a larger container filled with ice.

"Picnics—a lot like this one, back when Trace and I were kids. Fireworks, of course. And sparklers."

"Maybe you should have gone back home to be with family today," Penny said with a smile as she laid out paper plates. "We could've managed. But we're sure glad you're here."

"I had to teach yesterday and figured I needed the hours of working here. I'm not sure I feel much like celebrating this year, anyway. Not after...what happened to Billy." She bit her lower lip as she glanced toward the woods where he'd been found. "It still doesn't seem real."

Logan watched the range of emotions play across her face. She looked so vulnerable that he wanted to pull her into his arms for a long, comforting hug. "I'm sure it doesn't."

By all rights, the man who'd been killed should have made it to old age, and no one should now have to live with the memories of seeing that grisly murder scene out in the woods—especially someone who had once loved him. Good marriage or bad, it had to be the stuff of nightmares. Even Logan had awakened at night, reliving the moment of shock when he'd first seen the man lying in a pool of blood, and he'd only met Billy once. So how did Carrie feel?

Penny surveyed the food on the table. "Looks like everything's ready—let's eat."

They all sat at the picnic table and served themselves family style. When Carrie brought out a streusel-topped peach pie and ice cream, they moved over to the blazing campfire Logan had started while Carrie and Penny were clearing the picnic table.

"I've been doing some checking around town, over the past couple of days. Talking to people," he said.

Carrie stilled, her face pale. "Any luck?"

He flicked a glance at Penny. "We've both been trying to find out if anyone saw Billy lurking around town, or if they saw him talking to anyone in particular. No luck so far."

"And no word about any abandoned campsites, either," Penny added. "A deputy found his pickup with just a blanket and duffel bag in it, but it didn't have a camper on top. There's no record of him checking into any cabins, motels or resorts in the area, either. So he figures Billy must've been camping somewhere."

Logan thought for a minute. "If he did, maybe there'd be clues left behind about who would want to kill him, and why."

"You'd think. But the investigators have been searching everywhere without any luck."

"It doesn't surprise me." Carrie pushed at her

piece of apple pie without taking a bite. "He probably slept in the cab of his pickup. He did that plenty of times when he was rodeoing and said it saved a lot of motel bills. Though he did start keeping one of those high-tech backpacking tents behind the seat of his truck. A red one, I think."

"You should call the sheriff's office and let them know."

She smiled sadly. "I'll do that, though he was never one for backpacking and camping, really. I think he won the tent from someone in a card game and just forgot he had it back there."

Twilight had fallen and embers from the fire crackled and shot upward like fireflies into the darkening sky when Logan stirred the logs with an iron poker. "Anyone up for fireworks? They ought to start in a half hour or so."

Carrie looked up in surprise. "Wouldn't they be half over by the time we got there?"

"We have a better place to watch. Quite a few townsfolk come up into the foothills, too—just a couple miles this side of Granite Falls. Do you two want to go?"

Penny finished the last bite of her dessert and gave a blissful sigh. "That pie was perfect, but now I just want to clean up here and then head off to bed. I'm beat."

"Carrie?"

She glanced uncertainly between them. "You're sure you don't want to go, Penny?"

"You two should go and have some fun." Penny stood and gathered up some of the leftovers, then looked across the table and must have caught Carrie's hesitance, because she smiled. "Well…okay. Maybe I'll stop there for a while, then head on down to Aunt Betty's. Deal?"

Logan found himself holding his breath, waiting…not wanting the evening to end. He couldn't hold back a grin when Carrie finally nodded. "I know Penny—once she gets there, she won't leave until the grand finale. Let's get this place cleared and bear proofed, so we can be on our way."

The scenic overlook on the highway to Granite Falls was certainly no secret as a fireworks destination. By the time their two vehicles pulled in, there was barely enough parking space. Logan motioned for Penny and Carrie to take the last free area off the highway, while he parked along the shoulder.

"Looks like we got here just in time," Penny said as she pocketed the truck keys and handed Carrie one of the three flashlights she'd brought from the boathouse.

"Or maybe not, given all of the parked cars here." Carrie dutifully followed as Penny stepped over a guardrail and started down a short path leading to a long, rocky ledge high above a vast, deep valley.

Several dozen people were already settled on blankets and folding chairs along the ledge, some with picnic baskets, coolers and thermos containers. The scent of hot cocoa wafted on the chilly mountain breeze coming down from the high country. Down below, distant rows of sparkling lights revealed the street layout of Granite Falls, while colorful points of light marked the motels, restaurants and other businesses in town.

A rustle of whispers, marked by a few louder voices, spread through the crowd when Logan followed and helped spread out a blanket on a section of rock ledge well past the other people.

"That's him…and to think he's out here, free as a bird."

"Sheriff isn't looking hard for anyone else. Sorta gives you a clue, doesn't it?"

"Makes you wonder what it'll take."

"But if they don't have proof, they can hardly arrest him. And if there's no proof, how can you even *suggest* he did anything wrong?" a softer feminine voice protested. "Now, just be quiet—the fireworks are starting."

Carrie winced and glanced in the direction of the voices, then turned to Logan as the three of them sat down on the blanket, with Logan in the middle—probably by design, if the smug grin that Penny flashed was any clue. "Maybe this wasn't such a good idea. If you want to leave…"

He reached over and covered her hand with his. "Thanks. But this is nothing new."

She savored the warmth and weight of his large,

strong hand on hers and held very still, not wanting him to let go. "It still isn't right."

Penny leaned forward to peer around him. "The gossip never ended all last year. People were cruel, some were just snide—saying awful things aloud that we could overhear. And now it's probably going to be worse."

"Then maybe we should go."

"And give these uninformed people that much power?" She whispered just loud enough that the people nearby must have heard her, because they all fell uncomfortably silent. "Hopefully they'll be embarrassed and learn a good lesson when the truth does come out."

"Easy, Penny," Logan warned, his voice tinged with quiet laughter. He looked down at Carrie and gave her hand a gentle squeeze, then let go. "She's my guardian."

"Someone has to be," Penny shot back. "'Judge not, lest ye be judged,' the Bible says. And what about the Ninth Commandment—on not bearing false witness against someone? Some people figure the Lord's words don't apply to them, I guess."

Carrie looked up at Logan, wishing she could take away the hurt he must feel.

From down below came a distant thud, and seconds later a ball of green sparkles burst high in the sky. The crowd along the ledge collectively sighed in awe as it faded into falling emerald teardrops.

Carrie braced her palms on the rock behind her

and leaned back to watch as a display of fireworks in dizzying colors began bursting across the sky. On and on, until every color of the rainbow glittered across the sky as part of the grand finale.

"Wow," she breathed. "That was gorgeous. The prettiest I've ever seen."

"I think so, too. Without a doubt."

She blinked, suddenly more aware of her surroundings.

At some point during the fireworks she'd shivered in the cool mountain air and Logan had laughed, draped his arm around her shoulders and pulled her close. And without a thought, she'd snuggled closer and rested her head against him.

Now, she pulled away to look up at him and found him studying her in return, his eyes like molten silver in the moonlight and the dimples bracketing his mouth deepening, and she suddenly wondered if he'd been watching the fireworks at all.

She'd certainly been distracted by the lovely warmth of him next to her and the jittery sensation of awareness that had been dancing in her heart, than she had been over the firework display in the valley.

She glanced around and realized that the other people around them were gone, and just a few stragglers were heading up the path. "Where's Penny?"

"She left a few minutes ago because she figured the truck was blocking other vehicles. Don't worry, though, I'll take you home."

He rose smoothly to his feet and held out a hand to help her up. She ended up close—too close—and wavered between hoping for a kiss, and needing to step back into her own personal space.

The air between them felt charged. Expectant. As if the earth was ready to shift in a new and exciting direction…and then he released her hand and the moment was over.

"Um…thanks," she murmured, suddenly feeling a little shy. "This was a great evening."

They walked back up the path to the parking area, where a few families were still bundling children into seat belts. One of the moms glanced at him, then did a double take, and Carrie steeled herself for trouble.

But the woman just raised a hand in greeting. "Hey, Logan, good to see you. Say hi to Penny for me, okay?"

"Thanks," he called back. "I'll do that."

At his pickup, he leaned in front of Carrie to unlock her door, then opened it for her and stood back, waiting for her to climb in.

She hesitated, feeling renewed empathy for this kind and gentle man. "I was afraid there'd be a scene back there," she murmured. "I was ready to go toe-to-toe with her."

He gave a low laugh. "Now you and Penny both, I guess. Thanks—but sometimes it's just better to ignore those things."

"Maybe."

A faint smile touched his mouth. "I guess I just want the evidence to lead to the killer and the facts to be clear to everyone. End of story. I can't possibly stop what everyone thinks in the meantime. And to paraphrase Shakespeare, if I protest too much, it just makes me seem all the more suspect."

Startled, she turned back to him. *Shakespeare?*

He gently brushed a hand against her cheek. "I just hope this is all over soon, because I can only imagine how tough it is for you, not knowing what happened to Billy."

Penny was already in the downstairs office, getting ready for the first group of passengers on Monday morning, when Carrie tapped on the door and stepped inside. "Here's Murphy," Carrie said. "And I'm off to school. Tell Logan that I still do appreciate the loan."

"I will. He won't be here today, though. He has errands in Billings, and might not get back until late. He said to tell you to keep Murphy tonight, unless you're tired of his company and want to send him home with me."

"I'll be happy to keep him. I hadn't realized how quiet that apartment was until I had a dog for company." Carrie reached down to stroke Murphy's head. "My cat completely ignores me. Will you need me to work this afternoon?"

"Absolutely, since Logan will be gone. We could actually use you to cover Tina's float trips the middle of the week, if you could—afternoon and evening. And once Logan is cleared by his doctor, we'll need you even more, if he goes off to rodeo again." Penny looked up from her computer screen and leaned back in her chair, her voiced laced with worry. "I honestly don't know what to wish for anymore. That he totally heals so he can go risk his life again, or that he doesn't—at least until this season is over—so he has to stay here and be safe. But I guess it's all in God's hands."

After hearing about Logan's rodeo career, Carrie had tried to carefully distance herself, while still maintaining a friendly business relationship. But the more time she spent with him and his sister, the more she found herself being drawn into their world. *And* the more she found herself hanging on every word where he was concerned, wanting to learn more about this complex, caring man who had managed to come through false accusations and even a trial, without being embittered toward the community that had so wrongly judged him. A man who had shown her nothing but kindness and concern.

"Logan has never mentioned how he got hurt," she ventured.

Penny shook her head. "And he won't, unless you badger him. He's always been like that. Our dad tends to make quite a bit out of whatever ails him. Logan is just the opposite."

"Can you tell me what happened?"

"I'd normally just leave it to him. But he probably isn't going to, and you should know since you work for us now."

Carrie looked up sharply. "Is it bad?"

"Bad enough. Severe headaches. Lower back pain like no other. That's why he's our last resort as a raft guide, but you won't ever hear him complain. He doesn't talk much about his success, either. Two years ago he was the reserve national saddle bronc champion. Not that he was after the glory, but he has tremendous drive and determination, and every win helped our parents get back on their feet." Penny's voice hardened. "Last year, of course, he was out much of the season because of the trial. I still can't believe he had to go through all of that based on such circumstantial evidence."

"After getting to know him, I can't, either. And I wasn't even here."

"This year he wanted a stellar year on the circuit. We could use the money. But he drew a rank bronc at his first rodeo. He made it to the eight-second buzzer, but got hung up in the saddle, and the pickup men didn't get there in time. The horse doubled back and crashed into the chutes, then kicked him in the head and lower back while scrambling to its feet."

Carrie felt a sudden wave of nausea, knowing the tremendous power of a panicking horse. The terrible damage one could inflict.

"He received a severe concussion, needless to say—and a hairline crack at the back of his skull.

A few millimeters difference, and the docs say he would've been killed instantly. A couple of vertebrae were damaged. It's why he only takes float trips when he has to and wears a back brace under his life jacket. You can bet that he's taking Ibuprofen for a couple days after."

"And he wants to go *back* to rodeo?"

"He's sure that the longer he's out, the more he'll lose his skill and sense of timing, and after his legal expenses last year he wants to get back on solid financial ground. But the docs say another head injury—even minor—could result in permanent disabilities. The same with his back—it's weaker now, and causes him a lot of pain. Even if he uses a brace, he could damage it further if he goes back to bronc riding."

"Then it's crazy to take the risk."

"But try to talk him out of it," Penny retorted. "I sure have."

Carrie nodded. "I dealt with Billy long enough to know it didn't do much good. Only in his case, he never did do all that well and the entire venture kept us in the red, year after next. He was always sure the pot of gold was right around the corner and wouldn't quit. In his case, I think it was more of a Peter Pan syndrome."

"Not all cowboys are like that."

Carrie tried for a smile. "I know. For most, it's a professional sport and they work as hard at it as any athlete. But Billy wanted the life of irresponsibility and being able to take off with his carefree buddies for months on end. And it wasn't just that. Whenever he was off chasing his dreams, my heart would nearly stop whenever the phone rang. I was so afraid I'd hear that he'd been badly injured. Or killed. I could never go through that again."

Penny nodded. "I love rodeo. I used to be a barrel racer, before my parents lost the ranch, so I have nothing against the sport. But Logan pursues it because of his stubborn sense of responsibility, and apparently Billy pursued it so he wouldn't have to grow up. Both of them would have been better off if they'd just stayed home."

FIFTEEN

On Tuesday afternoon, Carrie showed up for work as usual at one o'clock. After glancing into the office, she spied Logan and Penny by the boathouse and waved.

Logan watched her as she sauntered over. The cuffs of her bright red, open collared shirt were rolled back, and with her slim white jeans she looked as pretty and fresh as the bright poppies growing near the river's edge, though the signs of strain still showed in her sad eyes. No wonder, with the murder of her ex-husband still unresolved.

"Hey, guys. How is everything?"

Penny glanced at Logan, then shook her head. "I guess you've got a day off. We had four groups cancel today...plus eight individual reservations. We have just one float that's half-full, Logan will be guiding a group of fly fishermen from Ohio on Wednesday. We hope."

Carrie's eyes widened. "Yesterday there was just one cancellation."

"Right—so I guess the first two weeks after the murder were slower, but now the word must be starting to spread. I suppose tourists stop at a gas station or gift shop or café on their way up here, hear the latest news in Granite Falls, and decide to pull out." Penny scooped a mass of auburn curls away from her face. "We went through this last year, too, and business was slow all year. Obviously, any association with murder is a major turnoff, and I don't blame them."

"I just don't understand any of this," Carrie said glumly, staring out at the river. "Why was Billy out here that Friday night, when I'd already made it clear that I wouldn't give him any money? He was obviously intimidated by Logan, so why would he risk another encounter? And why would anyone kill him? He had his faults, but…"

"Maybe the BCI investigators will turn up something," Penny said. "I heard that they've questioned the people who saw us with Billy in town. And surely they've traced his footsteps back to wherever he came from before he arrived in town, right?"

"I hope so. And what about any suspects? Surely there must be others besides us."

"If there were, we'd be the last ones privy to *that* news. Believe me."

"I still wonder about Dante. No matter what you say, owning guns, his military background and having significant mental issues make him suspicious in my book."

Penny nodded slowly. "Yet he's never been in trouble around here, and there'd be the question of motive. When would he have ever had any interaction with Billy?"

"Does he has PTSD? Would he try to defend his territory?"

"PTSD, yes. Would he go into crazy defense mode? I don't know."

"If it isn't him, who else would do it?" Carrie's voice trembled. "Who could be so motivated that they'd pull a trigger *twice?*"

"Other than you and I?" Logan held back a bitter laugh, remembering how public opinion had surged against him last year. "We're probably the key suspects to everyone around here. You, as the frightened ex-wife, and me with my supposed history of violence."

"People were still talking about Billy's murder at church Sunday, but they weren't blaming you. There was more concern about the fact that a killer is still on the loose. Who knows—he might still be in the area, looking for another victim."

He felt a flicker of surprise at that, and apparently she noticed because a smile touched the corners of her mouth.

"The pastor even reminded everyone to avoid judgment as part of his sermon." Carrie tipped her head and gave him a curious look. "You don't attend church at all?"

"Sometimes. Penny and I grew up in a church-going family. We had to be there rain or shine, or my dad needed a good reason why. But she goes now and I don't…much."

"What happened? If you don't mind me asking, that is."

He thought back over his life, sorting through the twists and turns, the unanswered prayers. The terrible injustice of Janie's death and the loss of the perfect life they could have had together. His mother's suffering while she battled cancer. The death of a rodeo buddy when a split-second difference could have made all the difference.

Too many other events to count.

"I guess I just fell away. A few years ago I got involved with Cowboys for Christ on the rodeo circuit, and it felt like I was coming home to what was real," he admitted. "But then last year…"

"A lot of people cling to their faith during hard times," Carrie said gently. "They don't walk away."

"I didn't intend to. But emotions ran high around here. Just arriving at church set people off, and it was pretty clear that a lot of them felt uncomfortable having someone like me in their midst. Maybe God can forgive, but the good people of Granite Falls are better at making snap judgments and clinging to them no matter what the facts are."

"Maybe you *think* that. But that isn't how it is—at least not now."

"Though the longer it takes for an arrest, the more time people have time to think."

"But as they get to know you better, they'll *see* that you aren't the kind of guy who could hurt anyone, Logan."

"Right."

She frowned at him. "I don't know about you, but I don't want to sit back and wait for answers."

"Neither do I."

"So what do you think about Dante?"

"I'm going to find him—or at least try. I don't think he did it, but he does have an uncanny awareness about what goes on in these mountains. He's too wary to ever come forward with information. If the investigators questioned him I doubt he would've said a word to them. But maybe he saw or heard something that might help."

She nodded decisively. "I want to come, too."

"No. It's rugged out there. I might end up having to stay out several nights, just trying to find him."

"What you're really saying is that you don't think I can keep up."

She had such a competitive gleam in her eyes that he had to choke back a laugh. "Well..."

"If I fall behind, don't worry about it. I can handle myself out here. But I have a lot at stake, too, and I *need* to be doing something. Please, let me come along."

By midafternoon they'd reached a crumbling cabin upriver where Dante often holed up for the winter. It was empty, its sagging door wide-open to any wildlife that might wander by, and there were cans of food on the bowed wooden shelves along one wall. A dirty, battered tin plate and utensils sat in a washtub on a counter that apparently sufficed as a kitchen. Through an open doorway into the back of the cabin, she could see a swaybacked bed piled with moth-eaten blankets.

"This guy knows the woods," Carrie said. "He'd never leave his door wide-open and food residue around to lure the bears. He must have left in a hurry."

Logan surveyed the interior of the cabin. "And maybe he didn't plan to come back. I don't see any weapons, his axe or a saw in here. Essential things for survival." He nodded toward a row of empty pegs next to the door. "His heavy coats are gone, too."

"Maybe he did see something he shouldn't have."

Carrie stepped outside and studied the ground. Large, indistinct footsteps milled all around the campsite. Soft-edged tracks, maybe from worn-out sneakers or aged boots that were nearly worn through. But here and there she saw smaller tracks with crisp, sharp edges. Tracks in places she and Logan hadn't crossed.

"Take a look at this," she called out. "I think someone else was here."

He hunkered down to take a look. "Looks like

newer, hard-soled oxfords or loafers. Definitely not sneakers or the heavy lugs on hiking boots."

"I'd guess maybe the sheriff and his deputies were out here to find him. Either they nabbed him and took him in for questioning again, or he slipped out into the woods. He would've heard them coming through the brush, though. There's not even a good path leading up here."

Logan looked at her with a wry smile of admiration. "I guess you *have* spent time in the mountains."

"A little. So where does Dante go when he isn't here?"

"There are abandoned cabins scattered here and there. There's little left of most of them—maybe not even a roof. Some, probably only Dante knows about because they're hidden so well." He frowned. "And there are caves. Maybe a half-dozen along Wolf River, and more when you get higher up into the mountains. It will take days to reach even half of the ones I know about. I can get you back down to the raft office, first."

"We've got a good seven hours of daylight. We can separate and cover more ground, if you tell me where to start."

"I don't like the thought of you being out here alone. It isn't only Dante who might be out here."

She waved a hand dismissively, then lifted her cell phone from the clip at her waist and checked the screen. "Two bars. Do you have yours along? We can keep in contact this way."

"No. Let's cover the river together. If we don't find him, then we can hit the upper elevations first thing tomorrow."

"I teach in the morning." Which was probably why he'd come up with the plan. "But I'm done at noon. If we use the GPS units I saw in the office, you could send me your coordinates, and I could catch up."

He did a double take, then grinned—the first brief flash of humor he'd shown since Billy's death. "And here I thought you were a townie, when you first showed up."

"Never underestimate a gal you don't know," she said archly.

"I guess not." His appreciative expression warmed as he studied her, reminding her of that exquisitely gentle kiss and the wonderful sensation she felt in his embrace. It now seemed like a lifetime ago, with all that had happened in the past few weeks.

She firmly set aside her thoughts. "Let's get going. I really want to check out those caves while we still have daylight."

There was no sign of Dante in any of the caves within four or five miles of his cabin. Logan and Carrie made it back to the rafting office at dusk, and found Penny waiting for them, pacing the area outside the boathouse.

"Where have you two been?" she exclaimed. "I've been terrified that something happened to you, too."

Logan tousled her hair, and she ducked back, swatting at his hand. "We were searching for Dante all this time."

"Any luck?"

"We checked the caves, but didn't find even a hint that he's been there. Of course, he's always been careful to cover his tracks—even if no one is looking for him."

"Some people say he must've been in covert operations during Vietnam."

"Which makes it all the harder to track him down, unfortunately."

Penny bit her lower lip. "The sheriff and one of his deputies were here this afternoon. They weren't very happy to find that you two weren't here."

"Neither of us have been charged, the last I heard," Logan said drily. "So what did they want?"

"They were really insistent about finding out where you were, for starters. I think they seemed suspicious about you both not only being in cahoots, but thinking that you might decide to flee the country or something."

"If they think that, they're less intelligent than I thought."

"But it worries me that they'd even *consider* the possibility that either of you had anything to do with Billy's death. How could they? You have a solid alibi, with Aunt Betty and me. And I don't believe for a minute that Carrie could've pulled the trigger."

"Well, they won't find any evidence proving it, because there isn't any. So what else did they want?"

"They wouldn't say. But," Penny added, "I do have a good idea about what's going on, thanks to the local grapevine."

"Gossip."

"Not exactly. I've heard that the deputies and the BCI have been investigating a number of leads since Billy died, but they still don't have any good suspects."

Carrie shivered. "Which means they're no closer to getting the killer off the street."

"But it's worse." Penny swallowed hard. "I've had some phone calls from several of the people who were around when Billy confronted Carrie after the movie. They've all been questioned extensively down at the sheriff's office about what happened."

"That isn't a surprise, I guess." Logan rested a hand on Carrie's shoulder, knowing the murder and uncertainties afterward had to be weighing heavily on her heart. Wishing he could lift her burden.

"But most of them have been brought in a second time, now," Penny continued. "And the thing is, none of those people were close enough to hear Billy's demands, or to hear his threatening manner. And they couldn't have seen the rough way he grabbed Carrie's hand."

Carrie drew in a slow breath. "You're right. Billy was much farther in the shadows. They wouldn't have seen his expression, either."

"But one of them did say she saw Logan loom over him, and saw Billy cower. And the others arrived in time to hear Logan threatening to lose his temper. Ivy said she had to tell the truth when Sheriff Tyler pressured her, but she just feels sick about it, because she doesn't believe Logan did anything wrong." Penny looked between Carrie and Logan, her eyes shimmering. "And unfortunately, she says Tyler looked absolutely smug when she told him what she saw."

Logan nodded. "I can imagine. But just think about this. One small town, two murders in just over a year. What are the chances that there would be *two* killers here?"

"Not likely. And so far, no one has been caught." Carrie's expression turned somber. "I thought Billy was the one stalking me. Maybe he was…but he also offered to sell me 'information that could save my life,' and I didn't believe him. What if he really did see something—or someone—while he was lurking around, and that's why he was killed?"

SIXTEEN

Carrie tossed and turned most of the night, through broken dreams of Billy, good times and bad. Images of his mangled face. Their first date, when he'd been so courtly and charming, with that dangerous twinkle in his eye and his lazy grin promising fun and adventure. The leering, twisted face of Sheriff Tyler as he relentlessly pursued Logan and her through a nightmare world of eerie darkness.

The sheriff and his deputies hadn't been back since talking to Penny on Tuesday, and the uncertainty of that looming encounter awakened her time and again, her stomach twisting in knots.

The townsfolk who had described the encounter on the night of Billy's murder had spoken the truth as they saw it. But they'd missed seeing Billy's angry face, and hearing what he'd said. And Penny was right. Their testimony—if it came to that—could be critical elements in any trial.

Despite the warm sweater she'd worn to ward off the morning chill, Carrie shivered as she unlocked the door and walked into her empty classroom on Monday morning a few minutes before the bell rang. How had life suddenly become so complicated?

One silly, immature mistake years ago had set into play a domino effect of events she'd never expected to experience. A rebellious choice to date a bad boy no parent would approve of, followed by a difficult marriage. A painful divorce. The death of her ex-husband, who may have been a rascal, but who certainly hadn't deserved to die. And now she was caught up in a web of events and evidence that might even send her to jail.

At the sound of footsteps, she dredged up a smile of welcome and turned to greet her first student of the day.

But there weren't any students at the door.

"Ms. Randall, we need to talk." Ed Grover walked in, his face somber. He waved her toward the chairs set up at a worktable in the corner of the room, then shut the door behind him.

Her heart sank. The local newspaper came out weekly and the next issue wouldn't be printed until Wednesday, but no one in town needed a paper to stay current on what was happening. The ongoing investigation hadn't turned up Billy's killer. There'd been absolutely no evidence found by either the local sheriff's department or the BCI.

And since most murders were committed by relatives and acquaintances of the victims, suspicion would soon intensify in her direction. She had all three of the necessary requirements—motive, means, opportunity. Except she hadn't done it, and she hadn't hired Logan to, either.

Bracing herself for the worst, she dutifully sank into a chair and smiled at him. "Can I help you?"

He looked at her from over his half-glasses. "I don't suppose I need to tell you why I'm here."

"I suppose it's either about the Noah Colwell situation, or because my ex-husband was…" The word was still so hard to say. "That he was murdered. I still can't believe it."

Grover appeared taken aback at the emotion in her words. "Yes. Well…it's a very sad situation, to be sure."

"I still don't understand why anyone here would do such a thing. I don't think he'd ever been to Granite Falls before, or that he even knew a soul here, other than me." She shuddered. "And now there's a killer on the loose in the area. I'm sure the community is terrified."

He gave her an odd look, then cleared his throat. "The thing is, such events are rare in a place like this. In the past forty years, there's been just one other murder here. Our parents are, well, understandably nervous."

"Of course they are."

He fidgeted with his necktie. "I received several calls at home over the weekend, and three more were on my answering machine when I arrived this morning."

"I'm not sure what this has to do with me."

"They've withdrawn their children from your class. They all feel that, in light of the current situation, they'd rather not have their children here."

She blinked. "Because my ex-husband was murdered?"

"Some were quite vocal about their concerns, actually. And I would feel the same, if I were in their shoes."

She felt a sinking sensation in her stomach. "So these people are assuming that I was involved in Billy's death. That I'm not suitable as a teacher."

"No one is actually assigning guilt, Ms. Randall."

Yet. "But they are listening to gossip. Half truths."

His expression hardened. "I talked to the sheriff a few minutes ago. It's clear enough that there's an ongoing investigation. And until everything is fully resolved, your presence here is not an asset to the school."

"But—"

"I consulted our school district's in-house attorney, and given that most of your students have withdrawn and that there are possible legal issues ahead, we are placing you on unpaid leave. You can, of course, elect to simply end your contract."

She blinked as the enormity of his words hit

her. "I feel as if you're sentencing me without a trial, Mr. Grover. I haven't even been charged with anything."

"We have a responsibility to our students above all else, and the moral turpitude clause in our employment contracts makes our choice very clear. But," he added when she began to protest, "we are trying to be fair. Hence, the unpaid leave status… which is more than generous given the situation. And when…" he cleared his throat "…when you are cleared of all suspicion and the case is solved, then of course you may come back."

She sank back in her chair. Armed with a good lawyer, she could fight this and win. The district had no right to leap to such assumptions. There'd been no formal charges, much less a trial. But a lawyer would cost a lot, and her savings were slim. And with what might lay ahead, her far greater legal issues could just be over the horizon.

Grover had her cornered, and from the faint, satisfied gleam in his eyes, he knew it.

"If you'd like to gather your things, I can wait," he prompted, waving an impatient hand toward her desk.

Humiliated, she scooped up her folders of research on Western American Art and her personal items from her desk, gathered her purse and walked to the door.

She paused, a hand on the door frame, and looked back, her throat tight. "You know I could fight this, but I won't. Not now. But when the truth comes out, I *will* be seeing you again, with a lawyer of my own."

On Tuesday, with no class to teach, Carrie jumped at the chance to take a dozen scouts from an inner-city area of Chicago and two adult leaders on a four-hour trip. With one adult and six boys per raft, and the leaders actively providing local naturalist information to the scouts, she settled onto the center mainframe seat and concentrated on guiding the raft through the now-familiar channels of the Wolf River after letting the first raft go downstream until it disappeared around a bend.

Lord, thank You for this beautiful day, she said to herself as they bobbed through a rocky, narrow run in the river. This section was relatively calm, though ahead, there would be four exciting passages between the high granite walls of Bear Claw Ravine, and beyond that, a calmer stretch where side channels often offered glimpses of moose and bear before once again the river turned to Class III and, very briefly, Class IV rapids, and grew more exciting again.

Just being out here, concentrating on the river and away from her worries, made her feel free and renewed, and at peace in this beautiful place.

"Look up—eleven o'clock. The tallest pine, with the broken top. What do you see?" The leader in her raft was Joe, in his mid-fifties, fit, with a military haircut that belied the kind expression in his eyes. When the boys didn't answer, he added, "Who sees that flash of white up there?"

The scouts, all encased in bulky orange life vests, twisted around to peer up into the trees and broke into excited chatter as they searched, until one shouted, "I see it! It's an *eagle!*"

"Good eyes. Okay—does anyone recognize that next clearing on the right?"

A chorus of voices shouted, "Our campsite!"

She tuned out the conversation and laughter as she manned the oars to guide the raft through the currents, around some massive boulders and a snag of downed logs. She stood as they approached the faster, rushing currents to better read the river.

"Hold on," she ordered, casting a quick glance at the passengers seated on the high, inflated perimeter of the raft.

The current bucked and swirled, sending waves of water over the scouts seated at the front, and they all shrieked with laughter.

All too soon, the river widened and slowed for several miles of quiet current. "So, boys, where have you been and what have you been doing on your trip?"

They all spoke at once, each trying to talk louder than the rest, until she laughed and shook her head. "One at a time. Okay, let's go around the boat. Each of you, tell me your favorite part of your trip."

"Earning high-adventure badges."

"The bear and cub we saw yesterday."

"Driving out here." The smallest boy, with freckles across his nose and strawberry-blond hair ducked his head shyly. "'Cause of the crazy rocks at Vedauwoo."

"Ahh...the campground close to Laramie, right?"

"Yeah—some of the huge rocks are like moon creatures, or something. They're cool."

The leader chuckled. "We camped there one night on our way out here, and we didn't think we'd ever get the boys rounded up. They would have stayed there the whole time, if we'd let them."

"I know what they mean. Okay, who else has a favorite?"

S'mores and swimming in a pool at the base of a waterfall were the next favorites. The last boy who was the biggest of the six, and had yet to say a word, was sitting opposite Carrie on the raft and remained silent.

He scowled when the boy next to him elbowed his ribs. "Camping, I guess," he finally ground out.

"I know what Ian liked best," taunted another boy. "But he isn't gonna say."

Ian's ears reddened. "Shut *up*."

"I saw, too," blurted a blonde with glasses. "And I bet he's got it in his pocket, 'cause he was afraid we'd tell."

Joe's head jerked up and he leveled a steady look at Ian from across the raft. "What's going on here, boys?"

Ian dropped his head. "Nothin'."

"Ian…" The warning note in the scout leader's voice was unmistakable. When Ian didn't respond, the man frowned. "We'll talk about this privately later, son. But if you broke the rules, you know that you could be sent home."

A long pause. Then, the boy jerked a shoulder. "I didn't do nothin'."

"He stole a *billfold*. I saw," whispered the one with freckles. "It was close to our campsite."

"Did *not!*" Ian roared as he launched toward the younger boy.

Joe leaned over in an instant and blocked the charge.

The raft tipped wildly, one end rising high out of the water. Two boys screamed, arms flailing. Carrie dropped the oars and caught the front of their life jackets as they started to fall out, then she fell back, bringing them with her as she landed on the rising side of the raft and forced it back down.

The raft slapped the river, sending a massive wave of water into the boat…and just ahead, she could see the trio of boulders that marked the start of the next rapids.

Carrie grabbed the oars that had narrowly missed hitting the passengers and took a quick survey. "Everyone is here—now hold on *tight*. And stay seated, hear? I really want to get you all home in one piece."

* * *

At the landing site, Carrie pulled alongside the first raft and helped everyone out of their life jackets. Ian, his head bowed, refused her help and fumbled with his straps until he finally gave up in obvious frustration.

"These buckles are really tricky," she murmured. She looked over at Joe, who was directing the other boys up the hill, and nodded for him to come over.

"I know you all plan to discuss this later," she said quietly, looking between the two of them, "but this is really important because your campsite isn't more than a couple miles from Wolf River Rafting."

Ian dug a toe in the wet sand.

"I need to see the billfold, Ian."

He shot a defiant glare at her. "So, you gonna search me?"

"Ian." Joe rested a hand on the boy's shoulder. "You could be on a Greyhound headed for Chicago first thing in the morning if you don't cooperate. I'm sure the lady has good reason." Joe looked up at her. "Did you lose your wallet?"

Carrie debated about how much to reveal. "Let me see the wallet, Ian. I need to see the driver's license inside, for starters."

"I didn't steal it, or nothin'," he said sullenly, unzipping an inside pocket of his jacket. "It was in the woods. Nobody was around."

"Exactly *where* did you find it?"

He shuffled his feet. "The big boulders next to the river, close to our campsite. It was wadded up with some stupid tent and some other junk—shoved way back. There were a bunch of rocks jammed in front...but I could see the red stuff—"

"A one-man tent?"

"I don't know. Yeah...I guess. Nothin' worth taking except...uh...the billfold." His head jerked up. "There wasn't no money in—honest. It was empty already."

She stared at the object in his hand, her heart thudding in her chest. A buzzing sound filled her head as she slowly extended her shaking hand.

It was damp, the black leather deeply worn at the folded edges, slick with mud. She tried to quell the shaking of her hands as she took it from him and tried to marshal her numb fingers.

But even before she opened it, she knew...whether from some sort of residual scent, or a feeling deep in her heart. But she *knew*.

The credit cards, driver's license and cash were gone. All the rest of the detritus that a billfold tended to accumulate over the years—the ticket stubs and receipts and outdated membership cards—was missing, too.

But there was one more place to look.

Drawing in a ragged breath, she snagged a thin, hidden flap along the inner wall of one of the pockets meant for credit cards. She lifted it back, then awkwardly pinched at the edge of a faded photo, trying to snag it. Her head started to spin as the damp leather held on to it…then finally, it began to move.

If there'd ever been a question about Billy's death being caused by a random hunter, this would put those thoughts to rest.

Because this was his billfold, no doubt about it, and someone had tried to hide all evidence of his campsite, as well.

So who was behind all of this—and why?

"Yes, sir, I understand. No problem. Maybe we'll see you next year." Logan cradled the office telephone and looked over at Penny, who was glaring at her computer screen. "Another cancellation."

"I figured." She didn't look up. "Maybe you could give me some good news for once. I need it, because there's nothing I hate more than this bookkeeping."

"I see there are two more late July reservations that came in through the website."

She angled a glance at him. "Great. Until those people come into town, pull into a gas station or café, and ask for directions or otherwise mention Wolf River Rafting. Maybe we should just save everyone the trouble and add a line to our website, like, 'By the way, we're really nice folks but every year, the cops suspect our owner of murder. So when you arrive, he may be at another trial.'"

Logan set his jaw. "I'm not letting it get that far this time."

"On that note, I got a call an hour ago. The BCI and the sheriff have gone through the woods near that scout camp with a fine-tooth comb, and found nothing more than we already knew—that Billy had camped near there. Nothing that ties him to any crimes in the area or association with a bad element. Nothing that points to his killer." Penny's eyes glistened. "How can there be so many dead ends? Right now, I'd bet that our county sheriff is busy trying to prove himself right about you. Since we *live* on this property, I have no doubt they'll find evidence that you were in the vicinity of the murder at *some* point. With Carrie's shotgun still missing, how are we going to prove anything?"

"I'm going back out to search for Dante, for one thing."

"And if that loony old guy gives you a statement, what will that prove? A prosecuting attorney could blast his testimony apart in seconds, just on the basis of his mental history."

"*But* he has gone into hiding. If he didn't kill Danvers, maybe he saw something and he's frightened. If he could even give me a hint, maybe I can find out the truth before it's too late."

"That's our sheriff's job." Penny made a sound of disgust. "And I wish he'd do it right. The man should've retired years ago."

"I don't trust the Lawler County legal system to

get this right, either." Logan drummed his fingers on the desk. "Remember those articles in *Newsweek,* about how many people are put in prison, then exonerated twenty years later based on DNA evidence? When this is over, I want to push for a review of *all* of the convictions since Tyler was elected."

"And I'd back you a hundred percent."

He glanced at his watch. "That said, I need to get going."

At the sound of tires crunching on the gravel outside, they both looked up.

"That's odd. Carrie's not due back yet." Penny stood and went to the window. "And she definitely doesn't look happy. I wonder what she has in that box?"

He looked out the window, then headed toward the door. "I've got a feeling it isn't good."

Carrie had her foot on the stairs when they came outside. She backed up and rested the box on the picnic table by the door, then turned to face them. "Bad news. I lost my job."

"Oh, no," Penny exclaimed, a hand at her throat. "What happened?"

She pulled a sad face. "I have to admit that the principal and I didn't see eye to eye on a lot of things. But this is just beyond."

"Because of the murder?"

"Apparently gossip is really flying in town, and a number of parents view me as a Very Bad Influence, or something. Most of my students have been withdrawn, so it's almost a moot point. But, I'm on unpaid leave. Presumably until I'm tried, convicted and hauled away for murder—or so Grover implied."

"But there aren't even any charges yet!"

"He pulled out the old 'moral turpitude' clause, hinting that if I wasn't involved, then I might be associating with those who are. So for the safety of the children and to maintain positive influences for them, I shouldn't be there." She managed a faint smile. "Though of course, if everything ends up well, he *may* let me come back. As if I'd want to work for him again."

Penny sat on one of the benches and propped her elbows on the table. "That's just so unfair. You should fight it, Carrie."

"With what? I can't afford to." She wearily sank onto the bench opposite Penny, next to the cardboard box of her possessions. "If only my shotgun hadn't disappeared. Talk about a red flag."

Logan leaned a hip on the far edge of the table. "Agreed. But the BCI combed the murder site and far into the forest, plus the roadsides for several miles in either direction. They didn't even find any shell casings."

"Which make it look like either you or I might've used it, then hid it very, very well." She idly thumbed through the contents of the box at her side. "I am so going to miss my students. The scary thing is that I might never get to teach again. Even if I'm not charged with anything, I can only imagine what Ed Grover would say to any future schools looking for a reference."

"And that you could fight, too. He'd have no right to do that…and I'm sure he knows it, too. You shouldn't have to give up the career you love." Penny leaned forward and peered at the top of the box. "What's that? There—that piece of paper poking up behind the blue folder. Is that from one of the summer art projects you did?"

"This?"

"No—the one behind it. The one with the really fine detail. Pen and ink."

Carrie twisted the box to face her and plucked out a sheet of paper, and laid it on the table. "This?"

Penny's eyes widened. "*Brother.* Someone is into carnage here."

"I didn't realize I still had one of them. The older versions were in a folder that disappeared from my desk a few weeks ago."

"Someone stole them? Why? I mean, every inch of the paper is plastered with detail and this must have taken hours, but it isn't exactly a Monet." She peered at it more closely. "And it's kind of creepy, if you ask me. Who did them?"

"The boy's family is pretty sensitive about his emotional issues, so I'm not really at liberty to say. The student left them on my desk one day after another, unsigned. I was afraid that the level of violence shown might be an indication of an abusive situation. My pal the principal disagreed, though. He apparently thought I was nuts to be concerned." She hesitated, choosing her words carefully. "The boy who drew them is indeed…troubled. I understand he has terrible nightmares, so it's no surprise that he might express himself this way, poor child."

Penny looked closer. "Look at it—the only thing in color is the river running red, so I suppose that's blood. And those bodies…*eeuuuww.*" She looked away, then turned back and cocked her head. "Hey, Logan. Does this look at all familiar to you? Look at the precipice. And that waterfall."

He'd been tuning out for the past few minutes, barely catching their conversation. Now, he shook off his thoughts about the Danvers case and glanced at the drawing. "Kids' stuff."

But then he took a second look. Leaned closer, and studied the detail. The angle of the cliff, the comparative height of the falls. The largest corpse, among many, was sprawled on the boulders at the base of the cliff.

His heart faltered.

He'd been on the search-and-rescue team the day after Sheryl's murder. He'd been the one to find her body, and with nightfall looming and four-footed predators lurking in the area, he'd made a judgment call and photographed the scene with his cell phone from just one angle before a wave splashed him and ruined the phone. So he hadn't been able to call for assistance, either.

Then he'd struggled to retrieve the body, and it had taken twenty minutes to load it into his two-man raft given the swift, changeable currents and turbulent water at the base of the falls.

A massive grizzly had lumbered into view just a minute later, grunting and sniffing the blood on the rocks.

No one had been there to help him.

No one else had seen her body, sprawled on those boulders.

But the child who'd drawn this had gotten every detail exactly right—and given the gory details on the rest of the page, had been terrified and deeply disturbed by what he saw.

He turned to Carrie and fought to keep his voice level. "Who drew this? Did you ever find out?"

She bit her lower lip. "I can't say."

"You can't, or you won't?"

"I'm sorry."

"I *have* to know, Carrie. Tell me."

"There…was a lot of trouble over this. The child's guardian was really upset when I tried to figure out who did it."

"You had twelve students. If I have to ask every one of them, I'll try to track them down."

"You can't do that."

"Look at this picture—right here. And there." He touched the paper in several places. "This is no random drawing. This is Granite Falls, up in the mountains. The one this town was named for. The kid got the details exactly right—including the exact positioning of Sheryl Colwell's body."

Carrie drew in a sharp breath. "You mean…"

"I was the one who found her body, and I was the one who retrieved it—alone. If this kid saw her body, maybe he also saw her die."

Carrie paled. "How *horrible*."

"And the last thing a killer wants is a witness," Logan added grimly. "If he ever finds out about these drawings, this kid could be next."

"I…I…"

"If I were you, I'd be mighty careful about keeping this drawing locked away, and I wouldn't mention it to anyone else."

"I won't."

"And I'd also contact the sheriff and the boy's mother, because if you don't do something, and word gets out to the wrong person, the child's blood could be on your hands."

She shuddered.

"So," he said on a long sigh. "Are you going to let me know who he is, or not?"

SEVENTEEN

Carrie swallowed hard. "I can't tell you the name of this boy. Both the principal and his...his family were adamant about that."

"Even if it means the kid's *life?*"

Her last visit to Noah's cabin rushed back into her thoughts.

His father had practically slammed the door in Carrie's face. Linda had clearly wanted Carrie to leave and never come back. But had Carrie misunderstood? Did they know what Noah had seen and fear for his safety? Had they been *threatened?*

The first day of summer school the kids had all filled out their contact information on index cards, so Carrie could call their parents about any last-minute changes of planned outings. She glanced inside the wooden recipe box she'd brought home from school and sifted through the contents. *Bingo.*

"I'll call his house tonight, so I can see his f—" She hesitated, stumbling over the fact that Noah *didn't* have a mother any longer, and revealing that fact would give away exactly who he was. "His family."

"When you go, I want to go along. If I'm right, this boy is in danger."

"But *only* if the killer knows about the final drawing and actually sees how accurate it is. Right? And I won't let that happen. So he's safe for now."

"So who else has seen them?"

"Me. Marie, one of the other teachers. She's a nice lady in her fifties, and has lived here all her life. And the principal—who is paunchy and about as flabby-looking as a middle-aged guy could be. He's also a bit of a whiner."

"You said he's a difficult man to deal with."

"Not in an aggressive, dangerous way. I certainly can't see any woman wanting to have an illicit affair with him—or see him having enough energy to trudge up into the mountains and throw Noah's mother over a cliff. I hear that his wife rules their home with an iron fist at any rate, so she probably doesn't let him stray out of their yard. Not only that, but both Marie and Grover just blew off the other drawings as normal kids' stuff, and were incredulous over my concern."

Penny had been listening quietly, her eyes filled with concern. Now, her cell phone rang and she startled at the sudden noise, then glanced at the caller ID and took the brief call.

When she pocketed the phone, she looked up. "I told some friends that I want to talk to Dante, on the pretext of wondering about the best trails up to Sumner Peak. One of them spotted him this morning not too far from here, over on Liberty Ridge. There's an older trapper's cabin up there, right?"

Logan nodded, reaching for the keys in his pocket as he started for the truck. "I'm on my way."

Carrie jumped up. "Me, too—just let me put this box upstairs."

He didn't miss a stride. "It's better if you don't come along. Those are some advanced trails up there, and it's a long hike from the parking area."

She hurried up the stairs, shoved the box under a pile of camping gear in her closet, then raced back down to climb into the passenger side of the truck. Logan was already behind the steering wheel, an elbow resting on the open window at his side and the motor idling.

"Don't worry about me," Penny called out. "I'll just stay here all alone…and bored…and try to fend off the sheriff and his posse."

"If we're lucky, this will all soon be over," Logan retorted. "And when we're vindicated, we'll be back to being too busy to even *think* about being bored."

The closest parking area for Liberty Ridge was along the highway to Battle Creek. The poorly marked, rarely used six-mile trail rising above that point wound through boulders and up steep, rocky trails more suited for mountain goat than man.

At roughly the halfway point, Logan pulled to a halt. "How are you doing?"

She frowned. "This has to be terrible for your back. I'm more concerned about you."

"I'm good."

Which wasn't exactly true, but if these six miles up meant finding some answers, it would be worth every Ibuprofen and hot, steaming shower it took to ease the pain that would follow.

She'd brought a backpack with her, and now she reached inside and offered him bottled water, then took one out for herself. "I've got four more, plus a box of granola bars."

He grinned at her. "What are you, a Girl Scout?"

"I was. So I've also got…let's see. Matches. A two-man nylon tent that folds as small as a paperback book. Water purification tablets. A matchbook-size sewing kit, with scissors. One of those all-purpose, multifunction, folding Swiss army pocketknives. And…folding cups. Oh, and a first-aid kit. And bear spray."

Now, he couldn't help but laugh in appreciation. "How did you pack so fast?"

"Since I've been living out here, I just keep it ready. I go hiking quite a bit, actually."

He eyed the pack, which had to weigh ten or fifteen pounds. "You should let me carry all that from here on out. The rest of this trail is a lot more rugged."

"Nope. I brought it, I lug it." She studied him, her humor fading. "And you don't look all that comfortable as it is. Are you able to go on? You could wait here until I get back."

"Maybe Dante is harmless, but the bears aren't. Let's go."

He set a slower pace, figuring that she had to be getting tired, until he looked back and found she was right on his heels, giving him an impatient flutter of her hand as a signal to step aside.

She disappeared up the trail after that.

He continued on, tensing his muscles to protect the vertebrae in his lower back and counting the steps he took, one by one. Whatever progress he'd been making with his healing was being compromised, along with his chances for returning to rodeo, with every time he took over a white-water float or ended up hiking on these rough trails. *And then where will I be, God? Just another time in my life where things are going totally wrong, and there's no way to stop it.*

Twenty minutes later Carrie was still out of sight, but now he thought he could hear faint voices far up ahead.

The trail opened up into a small, grassy meadow strewn with wildflowers in a riot of color—blues, pinks, yellows, violets—set against a backdrop of the snowcapped Rockies rising massive and uncompromising on every side.

He turned slowly, humbled and awed by the

contrast of such grandeur and the tiny, delicate rainbow of flowers at his feet. The place seemed to overwhelm his minuscule existence.

Maybe a thousand people had trampled through here before, but being here felt like a message, just for him. *Be still,* a voice whispered in his heart. *And know that I am God.*

It was a verse called up from his memories of Sunday School long ago. And that he'd remembered it at this moment, at this perfect time, gave him a sense of peace he hadn't felt in a long time.

Carrie's voice drew closer, chattering words he couldn't make out, and then she appeared at the edge of the meadow with Dante following a few steps behind her.

The man's gaze darted warily around the open space, and he tentatively came forward another step, as if unwilling to leave the security of the forest behind.

"The trail passed near his cabin," she called out. "He says he'll talk to you."

Logan joined them near several boulders marking the mouth of the trail. "We've known each other for a long time, haven't we?"

The old man nodded.

"I promised him something if he'd come with me," Carrie said. She broke into her backpack and offered Dante a bottle of water and a granola bar. Then she searched farther into the depths of the bag and came up with her palm-size sewing kit, which he took greedily, turning it over and over in his hand.

"Something more if you'll just stay for a little while," she said with a soft smile. She sat on one of the boulders and leaned over to pat the next one over. "Here, have a seat."

He hesitated, then sat, though he looked like a bird on the verge of flight. The miasma of unwashed male and filthy clothing obliterated the fresh scent of pine and wildflowers wafting across the meadow.

"Okay, Logan—fire away."

"Someone was killed close to Wolf River a few weeks ago," Logan said slowly.

Dante reared back in alarm. "Wasn't me. I wasn't there. No, siree."

"No, we don't think you had anything to do with it. But we want to make sure the sheriff doesn't come up with that idea, either. He's trying hard to solve this crime, and so are we, but we need help. Did you see or hear anything?"

"I wasn't there. Somebody saw too much, all right."

"You did? You saw too much?"

Dante gave a hard single shake of his head.

"Someone else, then? The guy who was killed? Or was someone else there?"

Dante didn't answer.

"You've spent the last few months down close to the Wolf. I've seen you along the riverbank any number of times. So why did you suddenly take off and come up here—away from the good fishing? You had to have a reason."

Silence.

"Were you scared of someone? Did someone see you—maybe the one who killed that man? Were you threatened?"

"Not safe. Time to go."

"Please, Dante," Carrie urged. She reached over, put her first-aid kit in his hand, and gently curled his fingers around it. "If you can tell us anything, we'd appreciate it so much."

Dante silently studied the box in his hand.

"Please?"

He stood, started to walk away, his shoulders hunched, but then he turned back, his face filled with defeat and a touch of fear. "Don't trust anyone. Not even the ones you know."

And then he melted back into the forest.

EIGHTEEN

By the time they reached the last mile marker on the Liberty Ridge trail, it was late afternoon and dark clouds were boiling up over the peaks of the mountains to the west. Logan had slowed up even more on the way back, no longer able to tough it out and hide the pain radiating from his old rodeo injuries.

"Want me to go borrow someone's four-wheeler and pick you up?" Carrie teased gently, though from the worry in her eyes, he could read her concern.

"I'm fine. We oughta be able to beat that storm if we just keep trucking."

"So you say, old man."

"Wait a minute. I believe we have just a year or so between us," he teased back, though there was a lifetime of different experiences between them that made him feel a hundred years older, and he couldn't deny that he'd become jaded over the years. Their differences ran far deeper than something as simple as a birth date. "Just when did you become such a Pollyanna?"

"Roughly at birth." She jogged in place, waiting for him to catch up. The trail widened at the last half mile before the parking area, and there she fell in step with him. "You did a great job, Logan. This is a tough trail in anyone's book."

He laughed. "You were a cheerleader, right?"

"Nope. I had to get home to work horses and tend cattle, just like my brother." She batted her eyelashes at him. "So, want to take Penny and me out for supper?"

Just you, maybe.

He reined in that errant thought, though the idea was intriguing. A night out on the town with Carrie Randall would probably eclipse every other social experience in years, bar none. But where would that lead?

Wanting *more* of those evenings.

Wanting to get to know her on a much more personal level.

And between the two of them, it would be a toss-up as far as who was the most damaged and unready for any sort of deeper relationship.

He'd bantered with her on the long hike back, admiring her quick wit. Her ability to handle herself well in the wilderness. Enjoying her company a little too much. Caring…too much.

But she'd just experienced the trauma of her ex-husband's terrible death. Had feared being stalked, whether by Danvers or someone else. Vulnerable as she was right now, any sort of deeper relationship might spring out of all of those emotions and not something real.

And she'd already made it abundantly clear that she wasn't going to fall for another cowboy ever again, in this life or the next.

Though heaven knew he had his own issues, as well.

Janie's death still felt like a cold, empty place in his heart. He'd mourned her for years, and then he'd finally healed. But the vestige of that loss had been an ongoing hesitance over commitment compounded by some failed relationships later on.

Coupled with this second round of false accusations, rising public sentiment against him, and the very real possibility that Sheriff Tyler might manage to make charges stick this time, he was the last person she'd want to—or ought to—connect with at any rate.

"Wow. You sure have given *that* idea a lot of thought. Was my idea that bad?" She slipped her arm into the crook of his elbow for a friendly squeeze. "Forget I said anything, honest. I was just joking."

"Sorry, I was just thinking about other things. Dinner would be great." He grinned down at her, thankful for her company and these moments of setting aside the more troubling issues that were looming. "How about pizza?"

"Hmm…just you and me, maybe?" She was still teasing, but there was something else in her expression now. A flicker of hope, of vulnerability.

Just you and me were his thoughts exactly, even though he knew it would be a mistake. "You don't really want to pursue that thought, Carrie. There'd be no future in it. You deserve a lot better."

She faltered just a beat, and then she readjusted her smile. "Message accepted. So let's give Penny a call and ask her to meet us, okay?"

What had she been thinking, practically asking Logan for a date? He'd been kind, with his gentle, tactful deflection. But even now he probably thought she was a little pathetic.

She hadn't meant it that way. She'd simply enjoyed Logan's company and had wanted to extend the day with a quiet supper to discuss what had been happening lately. That was all. Nothing more than that. Really.

Now, across a table from Logan and Penny, with the Dixie Chicks blaring from an old-fashioned jukebox in the corner and the hubbub of a big crowd at the front tables wearing Granite Falls Baseball on their jerseys, she still wanted to slither under the table and die.

"So you found Dante," Penny was saying. "Was he any help?"

"He was his usual, nervous self." Logan took a long swallow of his Coke. "He didn't like being found and he didn't have a lot to say—and even that didn't make a lot of sense. He said someone saw too much but it wasn't him. He wouldn't say he was threatened, but then he said he 'had to go,' and 'it wasn't safe.'"

"And then he said the oddest thing," Carrie chimed in. "Something like 'Don't trust. Not even the ones you know.' So what does that mean?"

Penny shook her head. "It sounds like his usual paranoia to me. You two probably took that trip for nothing."

But it hadn't been, Carrie mused as she finished her slice of pepperoni with extra cheese.

She'd finally had an afternoon with Logan, after all this time trying to avoid him. And she'd found him funny and warm, able to give and receive the little barbs of humor that had made the trip pass more quickly. She'd enjoyed every minute and wished for more...

And then he'd made it clear that he felt no similar interest. *Ouch.*

"So what's the next step?" Penny asked.

Logan angled a quick look at the other patrons sitting nearby, and he lowered his voice. "We have people to talk to...a few leads to follow. Carrie and I are going to talk to that student and his parents, too. If we don't work fast and find the evidence we need, we could find ourselves being charged and thrown in the county jail."

"I agree. I haven't heard another word about the

investigation, and Tyler didn't come back again to talk to you and Carrie, like he said he would. It makes me think that he isn't looking beyond you two, and now he's working on building a solid case."

Penny's words replayed through Carrie's thoughts long after the evening was over and she was back at her apartment with Murphy, who had now decided that the center of her bed was his alone at night.

For the third time since midnight, she gently shoved his limp, uncooperative form down to the foot of her bed, where he served as a cozy foot warmer, and then she flopped back to stare at the ceiling some more.

Without her school salary or many hours available at the rafting company, she wouldn't be able to stay here or anywhere else in Granite Falls for more than another month or two. By summer's end, she had to find another place to live, another job.

But even now it was almost too late to apply for other teaching positions for the coming school year, though perhaps that would be a fruitless exercise anyway, with the murder case still up in the air, and with the kind of reference Grover would likely write for her.

Which left the offer Trace had repeatedly made to her—the little cabin on his ranch.

Lord, help me figure out what to do here, because

I'm at a loss and could sure use some help. And if You wouldn't mind, please give Logan a hand, too.

Carrie awoke with a sense of new resolve. She *could* do something. Logan was right.

If Noah's pictures had been a silent cry for help, then she needed to gently talk to him and make sure his father and aunt knew about the burdens he was carrying.

And if indeed Noah had been a witness to his mother's death, that could be the key to helping Logan straighten out his past troubles and fully, once and for all, clear his name. It was the least she could do before she had to leave town for good, in search of a job. And there was no better time than now.

With Logan off guiding a group of fly fisherman at several remote, hike-in streams for the day and Penny taking rafters down the river until five o'clock—the best day they'd had in a long while— she couldn't leave until after six.

Logan hadn't yet returned and Penny was still chatting with some customers out on the riverbank when six o'clock rolled around. Carrie debated, then called the nonemergency number at the sheriff's department. The office secretary said the sheriff was out, but Carrie could leave a message for the deputy covering that area.

She hesitated, then left a brief message on voice mail.

After writing a note for Logan and Penny, she left it on the office desk.

On the way out of town she mulled over what she could say to Linda. "Your nephew is in danger" probably sounded too over-the-top. Unbelievable.

As wary as the woman had been, telling her, "You've got to come to the police station with me so Noah can make a statement" would probably send Linda running straight for the hills with Noah in tow.

And what about the child? If he had to talk to the sheriff—or even a jury—would reliving his mother's death be too traumatic, too difficult for him to face? Could she even think of putting him in that position?

Following her previous set of directions, Carrie turned off the highway and followed a narrow curving road way up into the hills until it turned to gravel…then a turnoff onto an even more narrow, deeply rutted track.

It was dark back here, with the evening sun resting on the tips of the mountains to the west and its soft rays barely filtering through the heavy canopy of pines.

She passed several empty rustic cabins, the doors half-open and windows staring out at her like black, empty eyes. She shivered, wondering why Linda and her brother would want to live in such a remote location. Privacy was wonderful, in a well-kept place, but the abandoned cabins were eerie.

The trees opened up into a clearing, where the last cabin stood. She pulled to a stop. Started to get out, then hesitated, as a sense of foreboding began prickling at the back of her neck.

Last time, there were lights in the windows. The door was firmly shut.

Linda's car was still parked in front. But now the cabin was dark, its front door wide-open. She looked around the clearing for any signs of motion.

Nothing moved except for the breeze tossing the branches.

Had Linda and Noah's father taken him and left in some other vehicle?

Or was the woman hiding, at the sound of an approaching car?

Or maybe it was all more innocuous than that. Maybe they were all out hiking, and still making their way home. Or maybe they were in a back room watching a movie on a DVD, and had lost track of time. Far more likely scenarios than anything Carrie could dream up just because the place seemed so dark, so terribly lonely without anyone around.

"Linda?" she called out. "Noah?"

No one answered.

She took a steadying breath, gathered her courage with a brief prayer, and started for the front door. "Linda—are you here?"

The silence was deafening as she tentatively reached up to knock on the door frame. *"Linda?"*

The long shadows of sunset crawled across the clearing, casting the weathered cabin in dim light. Was that something moving in the darkness over there—a wolf, or a coyote? A man, furtively moving through the darkness?

Her heart hammering in her chest, she turned to hurry back to her waiting vehicle.

And then she heard it.

A thin cry…like that of a dying rabbit.

Her imagination—or real?

Shaking, she turned around to scan the cabin, the surrounding brush. Maybe it had just been the wind, keening through the trees.

Maybe it was someone wanting to lure her back.

Breathing hard, a hand clutched at her throat, she started for her truck at a run. But as she climbed behind the wheel, she heard it again, and this time knew it was no mistake. The words, now repeated in a weak litany, chilled her to the bone.

"H-help me. Please…y-you've got to save Noah."

NINETEEN

Carrie drove the Tahoe closer to the cabin and turned on her headlights, then backed up and repositioned the vehicle a few feet over, aiming at the weak cries for help.

She grabbed a flashlight, made sure her phone was still in her pocket, and warily opened her door. "Linda?"

"Over…here." The voice was weaker now. Raspy.

Taking another careful look around the clearing, Carrie hurried toward Linda's voice.

She lay crumpled against the foundation of the cabin, half-hidden in a tangle of brush, her clothing crimson with blood, her face and throat clotted with it. The dirt around her was stained dark.

Carrie took a sharp breath as she knelt at Linda's side and punched 911 into her cell phone.

"N-no," Linda wheezed, choking on the fluid in her throat and trying to catch her breath. "Don't. H-he'll come back."

"Who will come back? Who, Linda?"

"He…he's got Noah. Go—find him." The woman's eyes rolled back and she slumped against the wall, her breathing barely audible.

Carrie finished her hasty 911 call, giving the directions and Linda's name as she hurried to her truck for the simple first-aid kit she kept in the glove box. She jerked on her only pair of vinyl gloves, then raced back to Linda's side and tried to examine her wounds.

A cut trailed from below her ear to the base of her neck. Others—defensive wounds, probably—were crosshatched on her hands and arms, and there appeared to be stab wounds on her lower belly.

And everywhere Carrie looked, there was blood.

Opening the first-aid kit, she stared at the puny assortment of small adhesive bandages, two-by-two gauze squares and a roll of clingy stretch bandaging.

She grabbed the gauze squares and pressed them into place along the neck wound, using strips of adhesive tape to hold them in place. She added more and more layers of gauze while applying pressure with her palm until the bleeding slowed, then stopped seeping through the gauze.

She searched for the other wounds, wrapping the worst as best she could.

Linda stirred, opened her eyes halfway. "Noah… please go…"

A faint sound of sirens wailed in the far distance, though with the curving, narrow mountain roads, it was still a long ways off.

Linda's eyes opened wider in alarm. "Shouldn't... have called."

"You need help. The ambulance will be here soon, I promise."

"Don't...stay here. *Go.* Now."

"Where is he? Where's Noah?"

"Taken. M-maybe an hour ago."

"Who did it?"

Linda's eyes drifted shut. Heaving shudders seemed to roll from deep within her. Shock...blood loss...would she even make it until help arrived? Carrie sorted through the memories of her last first-aid class.

Blankets. Raise the feet—except with a heart attack. But with those abdominal wounds, maybe not in this case, either? She ran into the house and brought out blankets. Rechecked the wounds, then gently tucked the blankets around Linda.

"The...Falls," she whispered, her voice weak. "Noah—please, hurry."

Carrie rocked back on her heels, torn. Then she punched in 911 once again and relayed the situation to the dispatcher. "I've got to go after the boy. I can't wait."

"Ma'am, you need to stay there. Help is on its way."

"The wounded woman is Linda Bates. She's

outside, on the north side of the house. I did what I could, but she's hurt badly and I think she was left for dead. You need to get here fast."

She recited the directions once again for good measure. Then disconnected the call. "Linda, the ambulance will be here very soon. Tell me where I should go to find Noah."

The woman coughed weakly. "Stay...on this road. A mile. Signs—the Falls. Hurry. H-he said...j-just like your mother..."

"Who said? Linda—who am I looking for? Who took Noah?"

"D-didn't see his face." Her face was so soft now that Carrie had to lean close. "Mask. S-said Noah saw too much. Had to take...care. Of details."

Sickened, Carrie stood and stepped back, then briefly closed her eyes. *Please, God, this woman really, really needs Your help. Please protect her... and bring help soon. And please, help me find Noah before it's too late.*

Linda had seemed terrified because Carrie had called 911, and now Dante's words slammed back into her thoughts as she drove away. *Don't trust anyone. Not even the ones you know.*

She'd had no choice but to make the emergency call. Linda might not have much of a chance, but she'd surely die without immediate attention. But making that call had also alerted the entire area of the attack. Most of the locals owned scanners and eavesdropped on police and fire calls, day and night.

And it wasn't only the good guys who listened in.

Linda had been sure of it. She'd been willing to risk her own life to avoid letting her attacker know she'd been found and that emergency help was on its way.

Had she been trying to give Carrie more time to find Noah before his abductor started to panic? Was it already too late?

With just a faint wash of moonlight overhead, the forest loomed over the rutted track leading north from Linda's house, creating a nearly impenetrable menacing darkness that the headlights barely touched.

Leaning over the steering wheel to peer out into the night, Carrie crept forward, her foot barely on the accelerator. Here and there, pairs of eyes glowed at her through the trees, then disappeared. *Please, Lord—help me,* she whispered. *And please let me get there in time.*

She glanced at the odometer, marking the tenths of a mile slowly rolling past, then straining to see any signs for the falls. Up here, there might only be a small wooden sign overgrown by brush.

A patch of white flickered in the beam of her headlight, then disappeared. She stopped and angled the flashlight at it. *Granite Falls, ½ Mile.*

The road was barely wide enough for two cars to pass, but she pulled over as far as she could, the underbrush scraping at the side of the SUV.

Fear clogged her throat as she grabbed her backpack and climbed out, defenseless. Alone. The darkness fell like a heavy blanket in front of her now that the Tahoe's headlights were no longer leading the way.

She took one tentative step forward. Then another, until she picked out a narrow path toward the falls with her flashlight.

Move, an inner voice whispered. *Hurry.*

She edged forward, prickly wild raspberry vines tearing at her ankles; her feet bumping up against unseen rocks strewn in the path. Biting her lower lip, she picked up a faster pace, swinging her flashlight wide to avoid the larger boulders and downed trees. How far had she gone now? A quarter mile? A third?

What if Noah and his captor were off to the side somewhere, down another path, and she missed them completely?

The fact that she had no weapon hit her a moment later.

If somebody was on the verge of harming Noah, how could she possibly stop him?

Logan drove slowly through town, searching for Carrie's car. She *had* to be here somewhere, trying to talk that student and his mother into coming forward.

But now Logan had been up and down every single street and avenue twice—not a time-intensive feat in Granite Falls—without a sign of her. Could she have doubled back, and then gone home?

An ambulance screamed through town, heading up into the hills. Another hurt climber maybe... or some three-hundred-pound old fogey with high blood pressure on vacation.

Still, an uneasy premonition worked its way through his midsection.

He'd asked Carrie to check with the mother of the anonymous student who had drawn the picture. But she'd hedged her reply, answering obliquely to maintain the privacy of the student. Now he realized why. She'd had to sidestep with her answer, because the child didn't *have* a mother any longer.

Noah.

The answer made perfect sense. If the killer had forced Sheryl up to the falls and then pushed her to her death, her son could have followed, frightened for her.

A nightmare, from beginning to end.

And now an ambulance was wailing up into the mountains in that general direction.

Logan thought for a second, then did a U-turn in the middle of the street and pulled to a stop in front of the Daisy Diner's drive-up window and peered inside. "Hey, Marge. Do you have your scanner on?"

She bustled up to the window. "Sure enough. What's up?"

"That ambulance. Where's it heading?"

"One of those cabins just south of Granite Falls." She pursed her lips, thinking. "The Colwell place, I believe."

If the killer had discovered that he'd had a witness, then Noah's life was in danger…if it wasn't already too late. And now there was a very good chance that Carrie was up in the woods somewhere—maybe in danger, too.

He floored the accelerator, his tires squealing as he took the corner back onto Main Street and rocketed toward the road leading to Granite Falls.

He wanted to prove his innocence.

He wanted to see justice served, and a killer taken off the streets.

But right now, all he could think about was the pretty little teacher who had captured his heart, even if he didn't deserve her. And for the first time in years, he started to pray.

TWENTY

Carrie moved forward, her heart racing and her palms damp. A jagged wall of rock rose high overhead, blocking the wisp of moonlight. Coupled with the dense trees all around, she might as well have been in a deep cave as she blindly felt her way along the narrow path.

Please, Lord, please help me find this child in time.

The wall of rock ended and the path curved. And now the sound of rushing water filtered through trees, growing louder and louder as she pushed on through the tangle of overgrown branches crowding the trail.

A branch snapped forward, slicing her cheek. A few yards back, she'd fallen against a sharp outcropping of rock that sliced through her jeans and lacerated her leg, and now the fabric was pasted against her calf with warm, coppery blood, shifting and scraping at the wound with every step.

But none of it mattered.

A few yards ahead the trees thinned and the moonlight washed a small clearing with silver. Beyond, the forest and rock fell away.

The roar of the waterfall was deafening now. Ahead, glittering in the faint light, a wide mountain stream narrowed at the very lip of the falls by massive granite walls on either side, boiling wildly over the edge. A fine, wet mist hung in the air, glistening on the surrounding rocks and trees, and turned the gritty soil at her feet to mud. Somewhere far, far below, the water thundered into a turbulent pool.

She stopped at the edge of the clearing. Tried to listen for cries for help, anything, but the deafening sound of the falls obliterated everything else. As her eyes adjusted, she carefully scanned the clearing, her heart sinking. There was no sign of Noah. No sign of his abductor. She sank back into the dark shadows and leaned against the rough, wet rock, her heart breaking.

She was too late.

He cursed the car he'd borrowed.

His own bad luck.

The fact that he'd ever been so incredibly careless on that fateful day nearly two years ago.

Since then, his life had been one disaster after another, thanks to an ignorant judge and a jury of idiots who hadn't taken believable evidence as fact. But all that was going to change.

And the next time he decided to fool around, he'd go into the next county. Find some low-down, backwoods tavern where no one knew his face. Where a girl might be down on her luck. Grateful. And know how to keep her mouth shut.

Though if she turned out as mouthy as the last one, she'd be breathing her last—and he'd handle it far better than he had with Sheryl Colwell. Grizzly country offered nature's own handy disposal system, but he hadn't gone far enough into the wilderness with her. She'd been found too soon.

Live and learn.

The boy cowering against a jumble of boulders fidgeted against the duct tape that held his hands behind his back, his eyes wide and terrified above the bands of tape that covered his mouth.

Too bad.

Raising his arm to backhand the kid again, he thought better of it at the last moment. Dragging an unconscious boy would be more work.

"C'mon, kid. Hurry up." He grabbed the boy's elbow and shoved him ahead on the slippery path, cursing when the kid slipped and fell with a muffled cry. Once again, he hauled Noah to his feet and pushed him on.

If the car hadn't bogged down on the muddy road up here, they would have been done with this an hour ago. Instead, he'd had to ditch it, camouflage it in the brush, and then he'd had to push on by foot.

With luck, he'd be able to get the vehicle turned and headed back down to the main highway, then run it through a car wash so no one would ever wonder about where it had been. Not that anyone would ever think to question him.

He smiled to himself. It helped being important. Being someone that everyone admired...and trusted.

Soon, he would be rid of the final witness who could identify him. There would be a certain, satisfying poetic justice in how it was done. A perfect circle of events, and then he would be completely free of the past.

If scavengers didn't consume everything but the bones, there'd still be no way anyone could tie him to the death.

It would look like an accident by some poor, foolish boy.

Or maybe, like the grief-stricken kid had chosen to take his own life by ending it all right where his mother had died. *Perfect.*

And as with the deaths of Sheryl and the fool cowboy who had overheard a little too much, there would be pieces of handy evidence left to shape the investigation. It was only a matter of time before Logan Bradley was collared and brought to justice.

He laughed, enjoying the irony of how well things had come together. In a few weeks, it would all be over.

And no one would ever think to look any further for the killer than Logan Bradley.

Carrie's eyes burned with tears as she turned to head back down the trail toward her SUV. *Poor Noah.* He'd lost so much. Suffered so much. And then no one had rescued him in time.

From far ahead on the trail came the sound of a twig snapping. Then another, coming closer. She held her breath, listening, her heartbeat tripping over itself. There were grizzlies everywhere, outnumbering the local human residents three to one. The browns were an even larger version of the grizzlies, and neither would be impressed with her half-used can of bear spray.

But she had matches.

She slipped off her backpack and pawed through the contents until she found the box of matches and the bear spray, then she shouldered the backpack once more and searched for kindling.

Everything up here was wet with mist.

She spun around, surveying the options. The path seemed to end here. She had to go back, toward the sounds—at least until she could find something to burn. She hurried down the path, around the bend, and through the thick underbrush as silently as she could, praying every step of the way.

The pinecones and twigs underfoot crunched. She

spun around, gathering some up, and broke small, dead branches from the nearby pine trees.

She brushed against a steep rock wall rising at her left shoulder, and peered upward.

A bear could scramble up it as well as she could, but...was that a small cave way up there? Would it be enough protection, if she crawled inside and started a fire at its mouth?

The sounds were coming closer.

She shoved the bear spray in her inner jacket pocket and stuffed the kindling into her backpack, then turned and scrambled up the rock, feeling in the dark for handholds and outcroppings for her feet. The first ledge was just eight feet off the ground. The second looked to be about twenty feet higher. She poised for the next ascent.

And then she heard a voice.

A *familiar* voice.

Her first, illogical thought was that he'd come to help.

Her second slammed into her with the force of a fist to her stomach. This was no guardian, coming to her aid. His harsh voice was more distinct now. Growling orders, demanding that someone move faster, *faster*.

Dante had been right.

It *wasn't* safe to trust the ones you ought to...at least where Deputy Vance Munson was concerned.

But she suddenly knew, with a wild leap of hope

and relief in her heart, that he had Noah. There was still time.

And, by the grace of God, she'd inadvertently placed herself in the only position where she'd have any advantage over a tall, powerful man. *Thank You, Lord.*

"Move it, kid…or I'm going to knock your teeth in. Got it?"

Noah came into view, stumbling and whimpering, a small, hunched gray figure in the darkness, his jerky, panicked movements telegraphing his sheer terror. Five feet behind, his captor followed.

Carrie froze and held her breath.

Waited.

Waited.

Now.

Snaking out her hand, she blasted the bear spray in front of the man's face, her arm just far enough away.

Choking, gasping, he swung wildly with his arms, clawing at his face as a litany of curses erupted from his mouth.

The gun in his hand clattered to the rocky ground as he staggered several feet and then dropped to his knees, struggling to breathe, his eyes streaming with tears.

Noah stared at her, his eyes wide with fear as she dropped to the ground and hurried to him. "It's me—Ms. Randall," she said. "And we've got to run, honey."

She glanced back at the groaning man writhing on the ground. "Let's put a little distance between us, then I'll cut the tape, okay?"

Noah nodded.

She started down the trail behind him, then looked back at the gun at the base of the cliff. If she left it, they'd still be in danger, even if Munson couldn't catch up. She had no choice.

"Keep going, honey…don't stop, no matter what. I'll be right behind you."

He wavered, frightened, until she gave him a gentle push. "Hurry!"

She doubled back. Munson stumbled to his feet, wheezing, still choking on the bear-strength Mace. He fell again, then blindly clawed at a nearby branch to haul himself back up, his eyes still streaming tears.

Giving him a wide berth, she flew toward the gun, glanced back at him, then scooped up the weapon and spun around to race for the path.

But he was on her, one burly arm clamped around her throat, while the other wrenched the gun out of her hand. She fought back a cough at the peppery odor clinging to his flesh.

"Every officer carries a backup, sweetheart." His hot, fetid breath exhaled next to her ear on a low, satisfied laugh that ended in a spasm of coughing. "Now, we're going to follow that kid, and you're going to call him back. Understand? Or the first bullet is going through your shoulder, and the second will be through your heart. Don't think you're protecting him, because you can't. Either way, that boy is going to die."

TWENTY-ONE

Every step forward was painful with her left arm wrenched high behind her back. Munson pushed her on, tightening his grip when she slipped and stumbled on the slippery path.

"Call Noah's name *now*. I'll bet he didn't go far. He's probably waiting close by, afraid to go on."

She felt the hard, cold barrel of his revolver jam into her right shoulder.

"Do it." His voice vibrated with anger.

She knew he wouldn't hesitate to shoot. And once she was down, he'd probably just put the gun to her head...though she already knew that the end of her life was just a matter of time. "You won't leave any witnesses. So what does it matter?"

"Maybe you're wrong." He gave her arm a painful wrench. "Maybe you'll walk away from this, free as a bird. Now *call him*."

But if she didn't, Noah still had a chance.

Ahead, to the side of the path, she caught a slight

shake of branches. She took a deep breath. "Bear!" she screamed. *"Over there!"*

Vance's grip loosened instinctively as he fumbled to bring his gun up. She sagged, dropping her full weight onto his hand to break his grip, then she spun and rammed a knee into his groin with every ounce of strength she possessed.

He doubled over with a cry of pain.

She bolted down the path, not daring to look back, praying that Noah had kept running...and ran into a solid wall of muscle standing in the path.

A scream rose to her lips.

"Carrie—it's me. Logan."

She drew in a sharp breath as her vision cleared and she saw the rifle in his hand. "W-we've got to find Noah. It's Munson. He'll be here any second, and—"

Another figure appeared in the darkness, then another, their silver badges glimmering briefly in the moonlight as they pushed on up the path.

Logan set his rifle aside and wrapped his arms around her, drawing her close. "It's okay. Another officer has Noah, and those two will take care of Munson. His days of freedom are definitely over."

She looked up into his eyes, still feeling almost dizzy with disbelief. "But how—how did you know?"

"When I wanted you to talk to the mother of the boy who drew the pictures, you evaded the answer twice. I figured it must be Noah, because you sidestepped the fact that his mother is gone… and he is the child who has gone through so much tragedy. When I heard the ambulances coming up this way, I got here as fast as I could. It all started to make sense. The EMTs were just loading Linda into the ambulance when I got there, and she told me the rest. Apparently she's known for some time about what Noah saw, but was afraid that the cops wouldn't believe her…and that Munson would try to silence both of them."

Carrie dropped her forehead against his chest. "I probably set it all in motion when I worried about the pictures, though I meant well. I truly did."

"How can you say that?"

"Ed Grover is a friend of the sheriff, and they're both on the town council. I can just see him chatting about his troublesome new teacher and her 'foolish' concerns. Maybe Ed even took that folder of drawings from my desk and showed them around."

"Then if Munson happened to see any of them, he would've known that there was a witness to Sheryl's murder."

"Right. And it was my fault." She drew in a sharp breath. "And I made it even worse by making that call to the sheriff's department before I went up to Noah's home. I didn't send help—I warned a killer, and sent him right to Noah's door."

"If so, you only helped uncover the truth. I'm sure a lot of questions will be answered once they start interrogating Munson."

She shivered, suddenly feeling cold in the night air. "Poor Noah. Will Linda be all right?"

"The EMTs said that she's one tough cookie. She lost a lot of blood, but her heart rate and oxygenation were still stable. If you hadn't found her, she'd be dead. She's one very lucky woman."

"Luck had nothing to do with it. I think she was in God's hands, every step of the way."

He gently lifted Carrie's chin with his hand, and looked into her eyes, then dropped a gentle kiss on her lips. "I think all of us were. Realizing the boy had to be Noah and then hearing the sirens at that moment, I suddenly knew I couldn't delay a single minute. If I had…maybe you wouldn't be here. I don't think I've ever prayed so hard in my life."

He pulled her more snugly into his embrace and held her tight. "Let's go and get you into a warm car. You must be exhausted."

"Not exhausted, just relieved. And anxious, because I still hope to hear a lot of answers before all of this is over."

When Sheriff Tyler and Deputy Rick Peterson arrived at Wolf River Rafting Company at noon the next day, Logan looked up at the cruiser and felt an automatic sinking sensation in his gut.

Vance Munson was a smooth talker. Convincing. A longtime member of the Lawler County Sheriff's Department. And he certainly had a lot to lose. During the night, Logan had mulled over a hundred ways that Munson might have twisted the facts somehow, to slither out of the murder and attempted murder charges he deserved.

The presence of local law enforcement hadn't meant justice over the past few years, and Logan expected nothing better now.

He braced himself as the two men climbed out of the patrol car and walked up to the raft Logan was working on.

The sheriff glanced around. "Where's your sister?"

"Float trip." Logan looked at his watch. "She started upriver, and ought to be landing here in an hour."

"And the Randall woman?"

That didn't sound good. "She just got back from some errands. I believe she's up in her apartment, packing."

"We don't want her to leave town."

I don't, either. Since she'd announced her plans, he'd felt as if a cold, heavy boulder had landed on his heart.

"Is this related to some sort of trumped-up charges against her? Because if it is, you have no idea how wrong you are. She—"

"It's not anything of the sort. We thought you deserved an update, in person. You've been through a lot of trouble lately, and the department owes you both gratitude for all you did, as well as an apology."

Logan caught a flash of movement at the corner of his eye and turned to find Carrie walking toward him, smiling.

She drew close, slipped her hand into Logan's and gave it a quick squeeze before letting go. "Linda had surgery last night, and is doing well. Noah and his dad are visiting her right now."

"She wouldn't have survived if you hadn't called 911 and helped her before the EMTs got there. She said she was afraid to call 911 before you arrived and could go after Noah, in case her call alerted Vance to go back to finish her off." The sheriff studied Carrie for a long moment, then he smiled. "You're one brave woman, ma'am, going out in the dark like that. Not many full-grown men would try to take on Vance Munson."

Carrie wrapped her arms around her middle. "I wouldn't, either. But I had no choice."

"Fast thinking," Rick added, his voice laced with admiration. "That bear spray just about stopped him in his tracks."

She shivered. "Not quite."

The sheriff nodded. "Adrenaline and fear can overcome just about anything, and I'm sure Munson was seeing his life fall apart in front of his eyes. I think he would've killed you and the boy without a second thought. Luckily your friend here led us up there in time."

"I know." Carrie angled a grateful smile up at Logan. "Vance was just getting his second wind, and I don't know if Noah and I could've outrun him."

It all sounded too good to be true, the congratulations and the acknowledgments. There had to be a catch. Logan cleared his throat. "So what happens now?"

"We called in the BCI again, last night. Interrogating a suspect can be difficult. But a cop who's done it himself for a few decades...well, it ain't easy. But we do have a confession and he's still back there, admitting to certain details. We'll be filing charges of murder, attempted murder, kidnapping...the list is a long one. But after we build this case, I have no doubt that he'll never see the light of day as a free man again. With Linda Bates and Noah on the stand, he doesn't have a chance."

Carrie frowned. "You think that poor boy will have to testify? How could he—he barely speaks as it is. And the emotional trauma of reliving his mother's death would be too cruel."

"His relatives say he'll be receiving all the counseling he needs, for as long as he needs it." Rick looked at a sheaf of papers on a clipboard cradled in his arm. "The courts won't request his testimony except as a last resort, and then only if he's emotionally able. Specially trained youth officers will obtain a statement from him now."

The sheriff glanced between Logan and Carrie. "We need statements from both of you, as well. We'd like you to come down to the office so we can do it right and proper, with a stenographer and video. We don't want to take any chances with this case." His mouth curled in distaste. "I support my officers one hundred percent. But when one goes bad, I want to take him down."

Carrie bit her lower lip. "What about Billy?"

"What we've got so far is that Vance Munson was stalking the Bradleys—wanting to cause enough trouble to drive them away."

"But why?"

"Vance had an affair with Sheryl, and killed her when she started threatening to tell his wife. I guess she wanted to run off with him, but he refused. Vance has been in a perfect position to doctor or eliminate evidence, and planned for Logan to take the rap for her death, but the jury let him go. Vance was afraid that people would start wondering who really did do it, and ask too many questions that might lead straight to him. He wanted Logan either jailed or dead—just to put all of that to rest for good."

"So he encouraged all the rumors against Logan?"

"And he was escalating into sabotaging the rafting business when Billy turned up and caught him lurking around the Bradley place more than once. Apparently Billy got pretty aggressive—demanding money for silence, and Vance had to get him out of the way."

Her eyes widened. "Billy did come here after

money in the first place. And once he got here, he tried telling me he had information that he would share for a price. So you're probably right."

"Munson had the perfect setup just fall in his lap. He got rid of a dangerous witness. Killed Billy close to where you live, which then clouded the case and made it look like you and Logan were responsible. Logan's legal history and proximity added an even better cover. Munson was probably elated at finding such a perfect way to pin the murder on someone else and get away with it."

"So Munson did take my shotgun," Carrie said faintly. "He broke into my apartment and took it. If I'd been there, sleeping…"

"The BCI is dragging the Wolf River for it right now, a half mile upstream." The sheriff's voice lowered to a respectful tone. "And by the way, ma'am, the county morgue has released your ex-husband's remains. Unless you feel differently, his relatives in West Texas requested that he be cremated, and that the remains be sent back to them."

"I hadn't even thought…" She swallowed hard. "Of course. It's their right to choose what to do."

The sheriff looked at his watch. "We've got a meeting with the BCI investigators and need to get back. We just wanted to give you an update, but if you can come in this afternoon to give your statements, we'd appreciate it."

Logan nodded.

The sheriff cleared his throat. "And by the way,

we regret the charges last year. We were operating on the basis of evidence, but now it's clear that our own deputy falsified that evidence. You'll eventually see articles in the paper about all of this, and we certainly won't sidestep the truth."

He and Rick strode to the cruiser. Rick climbed into the passenger seat, but Tyler lingered at his open door, then looked back at Carrie. "I hear you're moving. I hope you'll change your mind—we need good people in this town."

Carrie offered him a sad smile. "I don't believe I still have a job. And even if I did, I'm not sure the principal and I see eye to eye."

"Hmph. I'm sure that's Ed's fault, not yours." He winked at her. "But maybe you could just last him out. I know for a fact that the old goat plans to retire at the end of next year."

Her smile faltered. "I still think it's time for me to go. But thanks for the thought. You've been more than kind."

TWENTY-TWO

The last Saturday morning of August dawned bright, clear and cool, a perfect day for a wedding. The small group of friends and relatives were gathering up in a wildflower-strewn meadow at the ranch, with a row of saddle horses and horses with buggies tied up along the trees.

A perfect day. A perfect couple. Trace and Kris were clearly so in love, so excited about this day. They both radiated such joy that everyone around them seemed to glow as well.

Carrie lingered by the gray mare she'd driven up from the ranch, listening to the laughter. Feeling such happiness for them both…and a touch of melancholy, too.

The past two months back at Trace's ranch had been idyllic. Fulfilling. She'd gotten back on the district substitute teacher list for the fall. She'd promised to teach second-grade Sunday school starting in two weeks. Helping Kris and Trace get ready for this day had been delightful.

But despite how everything had ended back in Granite Falls, she still couldn't get that last glimpse of Logan and Penny out of her thoughts.

Penny had begged her to stay.

Logan had wished her well, his jaw resolute and little emotion in his eyes. No wonder. After letting her know earlier that he wasn't looking for a relationship, he'd probably been glad to see her go.

Well, so be it…even if her heart had broken a little more with each day since she'd come back to Battle Creek.

But this was a day for happiness, not regrets.

She straightened the many layers of delicate ice-blue lace cascading from the waist of her old-fashioned gown, then picked up the hem and made her way down to the people gathered around Trace and Kris.

"You look absolutely gorgeous, Kris," she murmured.

And it was true. The halter neckline of the dress caressed her trim figure; the thousands of sequins and beads on the bodice and train sparkled like diamonds in the sunlight.

"I can't believe this day is finally here, can you? And it isn't even *raining*." Kris's eyes twinkled. "And your gift—it's just unbelievable. Managing the animal shelter so we can leave for a week is the most wonderful thing you could've done for us."

Carrie laughed. "I just hope I can keep everything straight. If I get too confused, I'll just adopt all of those animals and you can start over with new ones when you get back."

Kris leaned a little closer and lowered her voice. "I...have a little gift for you. I think. I hope you won't mind."

"A dog. A cat. Wait—tell me it isn't that macaw that just came into the shelter. He has a mouth like a sailor."

"I'm actually not teasing," Kris said drily. "And now I'm *really* hoping you won't be upset. It's over there—by that buckskin mare."

Carrie turned slowly to scan the lineup of horses.

The buckskin's rider swung off and moved to the horse's head, where he slipped off her bridle, haltered her and tied her to a tree.

"You got me a *horse?*"

"Not a horse. A cowboy." Kris fluttered her fingertips and hurried away to join Trace and the photographer.

Carrie watched her go, then looked back and felt her heart give an extra little hitch as the cowboy turned around and surveyed the crowd.

As if by radar, he zeroed in on her in a heartbeat, then strode across the meadow, his white, open-collared shirt accenting his broad shoulders and slim hips, his black Stetson set low over his eyes.

Murmurs rose in the crowd behind her as he headed for her, looking like a tall, dark stranger straight out of some Western movie.

He pulled to a stop just a couple feet away and touched the brim of his hat. "It's been a long time."

"Two months." *And six days, four hours...*

"Too long."

She nodded in acquiescence, unable to find her voice.

"You didn't return my call."

And she hadn't written or emailed, either, since leaving Granite Falls. She'd tried to cut the ties that would only make forgetting more difficult. But now, with him standing in front of her, she felt a rush of emotion that nearly took her breath away.

"We miss you back in Granite Falls."

"We?"

A deep slash of a dimple deepened in his cheek. "Me."

"You made it pretty clear that you weren't interested in any sort of a relationship."

"I was wrong." His smile reached his eyes. "I finally realized that I had to let go of the past...or I'd lose out on something—*someone*—who is an incredible gift in my life. You."

At the other side of the meadow, the sweet, pure notes of a violin began to play, joined a moment later by the haunting ethereal sound of a harp.

"Um—I need to go," Carrie whispered. "It's time for the wedding."

She started to turn away, but he caught her arm gently. "I'll be here, waiting in the crowd. But I need to ask one thing…because I don't know if I can wait that long to find out."

Time stood still as she gazed up into his blue eyes, mesmerized, as she waited, her heart in her throat.

"I tried to go back to the rodeo, but my heart wasn't in it. I came back to Granite Falls, and it was the loneliest place on earth. I found out that the school principal wants you back. Penny wants you back. Your new sister-in-law-to-be called me, and *she* thinks it's a good idea, because she wants you to be happy." The corners of his eyes crinkled. "But more than anything else, I'd like a chance to have you back in my life. And this time, I'll try to do it right."

She didn't have to think about it.

She threw her arms around him and drew him close. And when he lowered his mouth to hers for a kiss, she kissed him back, drawing him closer yet, savoring the moment she'd never thought to have again.

When the kiss ended a lifetime later, she looked around, sensing a sudden silence…and found everyone was smiling and looking their way. A smattering of applause arose, then grew louder.

"Oh, my," she breathed.

Across the meadow, Kris gave her a thumbs-up, then raised two fingers to her lips and emitted a piercing whistle. Trace waved his Stetson in the air.

"Showtime," Kris called out. "But promise me I'll get to hear about this later!"

"I've got to go," Carrie murmured, "but I'll be back right after I help those two get married. Will you still be here?"

He looked down at her, his beautiful blue eyes deep with emotion. "Believe me, there's no place I'd rather be."

* * * * *

*Be sure to look for Roxanne's next book,
SECOND CHANCE DAD,
available from Steeple Hill Love Inspired.*

Dear Reader,

I hope you enjoyed your trip into Big Sky Country with Carrie and Logan. I love the Rocky Mountains—the wild beauty of that part of the United States just takes my breath away. I have such happy memories of our many family trips out west. Being there once again, at least in spirit, to tell the story of this couple on their journey toward love and deeper faith, despite the dangers along the way, was such fun!

This is the fourth book in the *Big Sky Secrets* series. Though each book easily stands alone, you can revisit Montana in the previous titles: *FINAL EXPOSURE, FATAL BURN* and *END GAME*. There will also be one more book, as yet untitled, out in December, 2011.

I also have books coming out for the Love Inspired line, as well! *WINTER REUNION* was out November 2010, and *SECOND CHANCE DAD* will be out this June.

I love to hear from readers. You can find me at www.roxannerustand.com, www.shoutlife.com/roxannerustand and http://roxannerustand.blogspot.com.

Or by mail at PO Box 2550, Cedar Rapids, Iowa 52406.

Wishing you many blessings,

Roxanne

QUESTIONS FOR DISCUSSION

1. At the beginning of the book, Carrie hopes that she can avoid revealing her past as a woman who was in a marriage with an abusive and unfaithful man. She wants to leave all that behind and start life over again, without the past clouding her future. For a woman who has been through a difficult marriage, is it ever possible to leave those emotional wounds behind? Or will it tend to affect her forever? What advice would you give if you had a friend who was in a difficult marriage like Carrie's?

2. Carrie wanted her marriage to last for a lifetime, but tough circumstances—and the insistence of her husband— resulted in divorce. What are your feelings about divorce?

3. When Carrie senses a prowler outside on her first night in her new apartment, she says a quick prayer for help. How often do you pray? Throughout the day, or just at set times such as bedtime and meals? Discuss the kinds of things you pray for, and what kinds of answers you've received.

4. At the beginning of the story, Logan thinks about his sister's encouragement regarding his

faith, and feels that she should just give up on him. Given the various tragedies and difficulties in his life, he doesn't feel God listens or even cares about him. Do you know someone who is struggling with their faith? Is there anything you could say or do that might help?

5. The killer in this story murdered two people and at the end, is contemplating killing again. He contemplates his situation and blames much of it on bad luck and circumstances out of his control. Do you think a person like this can repent and be fully forgiven for his sins?

6. Dante is homeless by choice, and chooses to live out in the woods alone. Do you see people like this in your own community? Have you ever volunteered at a shelter, meal program or other welfare service for the homeless? How would you characterize the people in this situation? Is there anything you could do to help?

7. Logan lost a beloved girlfriend in a car accident, and it took him a long time to heal. Have you lost a loved one? What things did well-intentioned people say that upset you—and what did they say that helped? Has it affected how you try to help others who are facing loss?

8. The sheriff questions witnesses who were close by when Billy confronted Carrie and Logan in town. One friend later says she felt badly about testifying because she had to truthfully describe the scene as she saw it even if it didn't reflect well on Carrie and Logan. Have you ever been in this type of position—torn between telling the truth or a "white" lie—knowing that the truth might harm someone else? How did you handle it?

9. Noah has suffered the loss of his mother. Do you think children react differently than adults to tragedy and grief in their lives? Why, or why not? Have children in your own extended family suffered losses? What helped them the most?

10. Logan has been harmed by ongoing gossip in the community. Can you think of one of the Ten Commandments that addresses this issue? It's easy for people to slip into gossip when they get together for coffee. Is it ever harmless?

LARGER-PRINT BOOKS!

GET 2 FREE
LARGER-PRINT NOVELS
PLUS 2 FREE
MYSTERY GIFTS

Love Inspired.
SUSPENSE
RIVETING INSPIRATIONAL ROMANCE

Larger-print novels are now available...

YES! Please send me 2 FREE LARGER-PRINT Love Inspired® Suspense novels and my 2 FREE mystery gifts (gifts are worth about $10). After receiving them, if I don't wish to receive any more books, I can return the shipping statement marked "cancel". If I don't cancel, I will receive 4 brand-new novels every month and be billed just $4.74 per book in the U.S. or $5.24 per book in Canada. That's a saving of at least 24% off the cover price. It's quite a bargain! Shipping and handling is just 50¢ per book in the U.S. and 75¢ per book in Canada.* I understand that accepting the 2 free books and gifts places me under no obligation to buy anything. I can always return a shipment and cancel at any time. Even if I never buy another book, the two free books and gifts are mine to keep forever.

110/310 IDN FC7L

Name	(PLEASE PRINT)
Address	Apt. #
City	State/Prov.	Zip/Postal Code

Signature (if under 18, a parent or guardian must sign)

Mail to the **Reader Service:**
IN U.S.A.: P.O. Box 1867, Buffalo, NY 14240-1867
IN CANADA: P.O. Box 609, Fort Erie, Ontario L2A 5X3

Not valid for current subscribers to Love Inspired Suspense larger-print books.

**Are you a current subscriber to Love Inspired Suspense books
and want to receive the larger-print edition?
Call 1-800-873-8635 or visit www.ReaderService.com.**

* Terms and prices subject to change without notice. Prices do not include applicable taxes. Sales tax applicable in N.Y. Canadian residents will be charged applicable taxes. Offer not valid in Quebec. This offer is limited to one order per household. All orders subject to credit approval. Credit or debit balances in a customer's account(s) may be offset by any other outstanding balance owed by or to the customer. Please allow 4 to 6 weeks for delivery. Offer available while quantities last.

Your Privacy—The Reader Service is committed to protecting your privacy. Our Privacy Policy is available online at www.ReaderService.com or upon request from the Reader Service.

We make a portion of our mailing list available to reputable third parties that offer products we believe may interest you. If you prefer that we not exchange your name with third parties, or if you wish to clarify or modify your communication preferences, please visit us at www.ReaderService.com/consumerchoice or write to us at Reader Service Preference Service, P.O. Box 9062, Buffalo, NY 14269. Include your complete name and address.

LISUSLP11